JUST LIKE A

JUST LIKE A RIVER

Muhammad Kamil al-Khatib

translated from the Arabic by
Michelle Hartman and Maher Barakat

Interlink Books
An imprint of Interlink Publishing Group, Inc.

First published in 2003 by

INTERLINK BOOKS
An imprint of Interlink Publishing Group, Inc.
99 Seventh Avenue • Brooklyn, New York 11215 and
46 Crosby Street • Northampton, Massachusetts 01060
www.interlinkbooks.com

Library of Congress Cataloging-in-Publication Data
Khatib, Muhammad Kamil
[Hadkadha-- ka-al-nahr. English]
Just like a river / by Muhammad Kamil al-Khatib; translated by Maher
Barakat & Michelle Hartman.
    p. cm. -- (Emerging voices)
  ISBN 1-56656-475-1 (pbk.)
  I. Barakat, Maher. II. Hartman, Michelle. III. Title. IV. Series.
  PJ7842.H3334 H3513 2002
  892'.703'6--dc21

                                                        2002009114

Printed and bound in Canada by Webcom Ltd.

To request our complete 40-page full-color catalog, please call us toll free at
1-800-238-LINK, visit our website at www.interlinkbooks.com, or send us an e-mail:
info@interlinkbooks.com

CONTENTS

Without hope, we live on in desire.
                    —Dante, *The Divine Comedy*

The Village

The camp was almost empty. It was a Thursday, so there was no one in it except for the few soldiers on guard and a number of others who were on duty for the weekend. Among this second group was Chief Sergeant Yunis.

The chief sergeant woke up from his afternoon siesta and washed his face with water from the cistern. He prepared his glass of maté, picked up the maté tray and the kettle of hot water, and walked toward the shade of an olive tree. He made a small stone fireplace, just like the ones they made in the village every evening when it was time to drink maté, and lit the fire. When the water was hot enough, he drank his first round of maté, thinking about his childhood friends in the village. He felt sad and lonely.

"They are in the village now drinking maté under the sindiyana tree, talking and laughing—Ahmad and Yusuf Mu'alla and Husayn Mahmud and my brother Muhammad—they are making fun of Husayn. I wonder if they are thinking about me. Do they know that just like them, right now I too am drinking maté, even though I am so far away from them? Do they know that I am in a camp in an olive grove, just as though I were in the village?

"I must return to the village soon. *Inshallah*, the house will be finished. *Inshallah*, Muhsin will return from Russia after he graduates. *Inshallah*, Dallal will also graduate from college and find a respectable boy from our area to marry. Ustaz Yusuf is a fine young man; he will leave Yabrud and go to Tartus, and we will all live between Tartus and the village. I will do administrative work at Muhsin's clinic; I will do any type of work for my son. I will work the land, plant olive

1

trees, help Muhsin. Ali will have grown up—he is my favorite. And Muhammad… Muhammad is the only one who doesn't like to study. What do we people from the countryside have but education? We are not…"

He drank his fourth glass of maté and was overcome by powerful pangs of loneliness. It occurred to him that maté had no taste unless it was drunk with other human beings; it had no taste at all when a person was alone. He spied a soldier going from one tent to another.

"Shamdin, Shamdin, come here."

"Yes, sir," the soldier answered cautiously, thinking that the chief sergeant was going to ask him for a favor.

"Come here, young man, come and drink a glass of maté." The soldier was surprised and tried to excuse himself, but the chief sergeant insisted.

"Yes, sir. What is it, sir?"

"Come here. Taste it, taste it—this is maté. They don't have it where you're from in Afrin." The soldier sat down and drank the maté as if he were obeying a military order. The chief sergeant felt relaxed with the soldier and asked him, "What do you do in civilian life?"

"I don't do anything."

"Nothing at all?"

"I farm and work the land. My family owns a small plot of land," the soldier replied humbly. He thought the chief sergeant was going to ask him if he could bring him something from his village. All of his friends who had done their military service had warned him in advance about chief sergeants, and here this chief sergeant was asking him what he did for a living.

"Ah, a farmer. In Afrin you have olives, just as we do in Tartus."

The soldier thought that the chief sergeant was definitely going to ask him to bring him a *tenekeh* of olive oil. He cursed the moment he had sat down and drunk this bitter drink. "Actually my family does not have many olive trees, and the harvest in Afrin was awful this year," he said.

The chief sergeant felt that the soldier had started to engage in a conversation with him. He allowed himself to relax the features of his face in the hope that he would seem less intimidating to the young soldier without having to announce this wish directly.

"I know—the harvest in Tartus was bad this year too." The chief sergeant grew quiet, as did the soldier, but the chief sergeant wanted to continue talking. "People don't care about olives anymore," he said. "They are all running after jobs, jobs, jobs. Drink up! Drink another cup of maté. At first, everyone finds it bitter, but after a while you get used to it."

He grew quiet again, and the soldier remained silent, suspecting that something was behind the chief sergeant's conversation with him and his offer of maté. Indeed, he began to feel certain that the chief sergeant would ask him for olive oil at the end of the conversation.

"So, will you work in a government job after you finish your military service?" the chief sergeant asked, wanting to keep the conversation going. "I really wish," he went on, "that we could have a lot of olive groves that I could cultivate—enough for my family so that we could live together. We have olive trees in the village, but not enough. I have four children and—"

"God bless them and keep them. How old are they, sir?" The soldier interrupted obsequiously, hoping to change the subject.

"I have older ones and younger ones. My eldest son is in Russia; he's studying medicine. My daughter is in college."

3

The chief sergeant noticed that the soldier was listening and not drinking maté. "Drink, drink up, the maté is good."

"It's remarkable, you seem like a young man, sir. Should I wash the maté cups and tray for you now?" The soldier had started to feel more comfortable with the chief sergeant despite his continual dread that he might be asked for olive oil. Maybe by washing the dishes he could show his appreciation for the hospitality, and in doing so he would have a reason to leave the chief sergeant.

With a hint of a coastal dialect, Chief Sergeant Yunis said, "No, no, don't wash them. Leave them. A walk is lovely at this time of day. I am going to take a walk." The chief sergeant was feeling bothered by being alone, and a sort of fatherly affection for this particular young soldier with whom he truly shared something in common began to grow. He felt comfortable with Shamdin and so kept talking with him, taking him into his confidence.

"I'm going to take a walk through the olive groves." He thought of asking the soldier to walk with him, but his military pride stopped him.

The soldier got up and walked to his tent, happy that he had avoided the chief sergeant's request for a *tenekeh* of olive oil. Meanwhile, the chief sergeant strolled through the groves, thinking that the soldier was just like him—he too had olive trees. Maybe the soldier's family, like his own family, was now pruning the olive trees in its village.

Yunis looked at the branches of an olive tree and broke off an old, dry branch. He then noticed another dead branch and broke it too. There was a big, strong branch that he tried to cut but could not. He called to the soldier, "Shamdin, Shamdin, get the axe from my cabin and come help me—the axe that's under my bed."

Shamdin came carrying the axe. "Sir?"

"You see, this is an extra branch. I am trying to kill time here. See? This is another extra branch, you break it off. See how I do it? I'll cut off this branch. The time for caring for olive trees is upon us."

Yunis and Shamdin began pruning the trees and talking about their villages. Two soldiers passed by close to them and saw them working. One soldier sarcastically said to the other, "Look, look how they are working. Just like they were laboring in their fathers' groves!"

Dallal

It was almost ten o'clock and Dallal was not home yet. Anxiety showed on Chief Sergeant Yunis's face, and he looked with an air of accusation at his wife, who averted her eyes to escape his gaze.

"Would you like some tea?" she asked.

Yunis knew that she was as worried as he was and that she wanted to keep busy. "Khadija, did Dallal say that she would be late?" he asked.

"No, this isn't normal for her. It's very strange," her mother, Umm Muhsin, answered. To calm Yunis, she added, "She won't be late, she'll be home soon." She looked at her young son, Ali, and said, "Ali, why don't you show your reading homework to your father?"

Ali got up to get his book. "Is she at Fawziya's, I wonder?" the chief sergeant said.

Impatiently, his wife answered, "I don't know. She didn't tell me. Don't worry, she'll come home. Maybe she is at Fawziya's." Privately, Umm Muhsin was more worried than her husband, but she felt that she should keep him calm. She tried to seem composed, but because she was so sensitive, trying to appear confident and patient was as much as she could handle. She added, "She's not usually late. This is the first time. She is busy with so many things, God give her strength. Her classes and her lessons and her friends and her reading—"

Little Ali brought out his third-grade reading book and started to read. Yunis was pleased that he read so well. "In our day," he said, as though he were addressing a man of his own age, "when they awarded the 'certificate,' it was a prestigious and advanced degree. They used to throw a party

6

for everyone who received it. A person could get a good job if he held this degree. He would become a man. Today, even a baby could get it."

Ali laughed when he heard "certificate." This strange word, he had not heard it before.

"God bless you, Ali. Get up and go to bed," his father said, looking at his wife with worry-filled eyes.

"And where's Muhammad?" he asked his wife. "Isn't he too young to be out of the house so late?"

"I don't know. I fear that child will fail in his studies. He's not diligent like Muhsin." She wanted to say, "and like Dallal," but she preferred not to mention the girl so as not to remind Yunis that Dallal had not yet come home. She added, "I fear that he has fallen in with bad company. I'm not comfortable with his friends."

"I'm in the army and you're in the house. The children are your responsibility! I work hard and I'm exhausted," Yunis said.

They heard the sound of the key in the lock. "Dallal—is that you?" called out her mother, looking victoriously at her husband.

Dallal came in laughing and walked straight to her father. "I'm sorry, Baba. I couldn't help being late."

"I told you not to be late," her mother said.

The joy on Yunis's face, however, was visible, and he responded to his daughter using her nickname. "*Ahlan,* Dallul sweetie. Hello." He stopped for a moment and asked himself if he should talk to her about being late or simply ignore it altogether. Before he had decided what to do, he heard himself saying, "My dear daughter, you know how much I trust you, but bad people, *awlad haram,* abound in this day and age, and many unfortunate incidents happen to people. This is a big city and people do not know each other here. I have heard about more than one incident involving taxi drivers and..."

He almost began to tell her a story he had heard in the camp about a young woman who was raped. But when he looked at her and saw her fresh young face before him, he felt uncomfortable with this topic. How terrible this incident, how horrific this idea was. Dallal could be raped one day or even killed. Somebody could mutilate her dead body, as had happened to the girl from the village Sheikh Sa'ad. He could lose her, Dallal, his precious and only daughter.

He did not pronounce the word rape but simply continued on. "Last year, I heard about a girl who was killed and her body dumped behind the dormitories on the university campus. She was a girl like you. She was out late and came back alone with a taxi driver. You know..."

"Baba, I'm not always late," Dallal said. "Only tonight. Today, my English drama professor invited all of the students in our class, male and female, to a tea party at his house. The conversation ran on and we stayed up late, completely losing track of time because we were practicing English. Baba, you need to practice languages, like you do reading."

Knowing how serious all this would sound to her father, Dallal redirected her words toward her mother. "Mama, is there any food? I got hungry after the tea. Those British are so precise! When they say tea, they mean only tea, and they don't give you anything to eat, except cake."

Calm now, Yunis got up and went to bed, thinking, "Dallal is a good girl and she should study hard. *Inshallah*, she will be successful like her brother Muhsin."

Dallal

"Hurry up, Mama. Hurry, I don't have much time, I'm late."

Dallal's mother ran about wondering, "Will any of them ever be satisfied? Dallal who is always in a hurry? Or Yunis who is afraid of missing his army bus? Or little Ali, or Muhammad, who doesn't like anything and always insists on sleeping late?"

"Tea, tea, where's the tea?" Dallal asked.

"Put out the olives," her mother said.

"Where's the bread?"

Yunis rode the bus to his unit and Ali walked to school. Dallal went to Dariya, where she gave hour-long English lessons at the middle school. As always, Umm Muhsin tried to wake up the sleeping Muhammad. She rushed to complete her morning chores, but when she saw Yunis walking out the door with a piece of bread in his hand, she knew that all her running around and her fatigue from having woken up early were useless.

This morning, Yunis stood at the door and lectured Dallal before he left. "Tonight I am on duty and no one will be with your siblings. You are the oldest child in the house." He said this because he wished to remind Dallal, without punishing her, that she had begun coming home late. He was afraid that his daughter would think he was saying this because he did not trust her, but he could not hide his fear, so he left it at reminding her that she would be assuming his position in the house.

As she was leaving for Dariya, her mother reminded her, "Dallal, don't be late. Today is Thursday. Ustaz Yusuf will visit us this evening, and I know that you two enjoy talking to each other."

"Is Ustaz Yusuf really coming today? I won't be late. I have three hours of teaching in Dariya. Afterward, I'll go to the university, and then I'll go from there with Fawziya over to her house. It's been a long time since I've visited her mother and her son. I'll get to Fawziya's before seven o'clock. Tell Ustaz Yusuf to stay a while if I'm late. I do enjoy talking to him."

"Your brother Muhsin—may God give him strength and bring him home safely—stayed at home more than you, even though he was a boy. Send my greetings to Fawziya and tell her to come visit."

"There is no difference between girls and boys," Dallal said. "Do we agree on that, Mama?" Then she added, laughing, "Did you have any new dreams last night?"

Umm Muhsin liked Dallal's friend Fawziya, who taught with her in Dariya and also studied at the university. Fawziya was older than Dallal; she had a child and knew how to relate to women better than Dallal did. Fawziya enjoyed spending time with Umm Muhsin and reading the future in cups of Arabic coffee with her. They talked with each other about dreams, while Dallal poked fun at them all the while.

"See you later, Mama," Dallal said as she left.

She walked toward the bus stop thinking about the hints her mother and father had been giving her. "They are good people and they trust me, but this archaic fear remains in their minds. However well-meaning and trusting they are, they want to impose their will on me. Their outdated mentality disrespects girls. That's Arab society. No matter how liberated people try to seem, deep inside themselves they remain profoundly backward. They always harbor fears about women—of them and for them. I do not know why they are afraid for me. I work like my father. There is no way anyone could exploit and humiliate me. Men in our country do not trust women because they do not trust themselves. Men—"

"Good morning, baby!"

Dallal turned and saw a young man trying to flirt with her. She turned away from him and got on the bus to Dariya, continuing her thoughts.

"These disgusting, stupid men. Not one of them ever looks at a woman except sexually. They do not want women to become liberated; this way we will remain their prey and servants. I swear to God, I will only ever marry a man who treats me with respect. Truly, I will never marry. There is not a man to be found in our country who respects women. None, ever. All Middle Eastern men are backward. When will they be civilized like European men? Like Doctor Morton White? He is so different from our Arab professors! I will live alone even if it means I never marry. Young European women live alone. They rent rooms and come home at night when they like. Over there, men do not harass women in the streets but are polite like Doctor Morton White. He is the only one who invited us to his house, a simple house. Even the Middle Eastern stuff that he has we saw with new eyes in his house. Oh, if I were only able to visit Europe just one time. If I could only emigrate from this country and be finished with this backward society. My parents are good people, but they remain a part of this society. The important thing is that a woman be able to live her life and have her freedom. My brother went to Russia and there was no problem with that. I'm sure that they wouldn't have let me go if I had received the same scholarship. Our country's laws do not permit a woman to travel abroad without the permission of a guardian. Must a woman have a guardian who is responsible for her? In Europe, women are responsible for themselves. In Europe—"

"Oh, I'm sorry," Dallal said, realizing that she had bumped into an old man on the sidewalk as she got off the bus.

"Don't worry about it," he said. "It's nothing my dear. Take care of yourself, daughter. May God cover up all your mistakes."

Dallal approached the middle school and, looking at the black door, her heart sank. "Everything is black like this door—the director, the students. Why do I have to teach while I am still a student? Why don't I have time to concentrate only on my studies and not have to prepare all these lessons? That's how it is in our poor, backward country. In Europe, a student is a student and a teacher is a teacher. It's too soon for working and misery."

As she passed by the black door, she saw students in a circle around Fawziya in the schoolyard, and tried to add some levity to her serious thoughts.

"Good morning," Dallal called out, laughing.

Fawziya looked at Dallal and swung her hair with an affected, coquettish movement typical of Arab girls, yet somehow her own. "Good morning to you!"

"See you later," she said to her students. Then, as if continuing a previous conversation, Fawziya said, "You were so beautiful last night. I've never seen you so dolled up before. Why don't you abandon your ideology—these serious, anarchic ideas—and take care of yourself more? Didn't you notice how the professor was looking at you? Oh, Dallal, I love you even though you can be stupid!"

"Shut up, you—let's go to your house today after school. I've missed Ra'id and your mother. Hurry to class—the students have gone into the classroom!"

Yusuf

Every week on Thursday afternoon, Yusuf came from Yabrud and wandered the streets of Damascus. He would search for a new film, a new book, or a gathering where he could relax after a week of work—a week of reading, teaching, and loneliness.

Even Yusuf's Thursdays, however, had become regimented: arrive in the afternoon, go to Zuhayr Qawasmi's place, decide how to meet up later that night. At three o'clock, he would go to the movies if a good film was showing, and after leaving the cinema, he'd browse through bookstores to see if anything caught his eye. After the bookstores, he would visit his relatives in Mezzeh—the family of Chief Sergeant Yunis Muhammad, a relative on his father's side, and whose wife, Umm Muhsin, was a cousin on his mother's side. As in every village, people were all somehow related to each other, either as close or more distant relations.

In recent months, Yusuf had started to be more inclined to visit the chief sergeant's family because he had started to have longer and longer conversations with Dallal. He had found himself drawn to her independent personality and her intelligence, as well as her continuing interest in reading and cinema. And he would have been blind not to notice her beauty. This evening he was determined to invite her to a movie for the following week.

Yusuf called Zuhayr the moment he arrived, and they agreed to meet at nine to drink a bottle of wine and hang out together. Afterward, Yusuf was to sleep at Zuhayr's place—he lived alone, not with his family like most other young, unmarried men in Damascus.

He walked over to the Kindi Theater and saw the posters for a popular, new Arab film, but continued onward, wandering aimlessly through the streets and thinking, "I've started to get sick of my life—these routines, lessons, students, Yabrud, Damascus—even weekends have started to become routine. Nothing is ever new, there is no new cinema, there are only streets, bookstores, and Abu Muhsin's family. Dallal is a lovely, intelligent young woman. I'm sure that she has a boyfriend, though from what she says it seems that she isn't involved with anyone. She treats me like a relative and a serious teacher. Perhaps she simply respects me as a philosophy teacher, as a reader of books. She is used to Damascus; she was born and raised here. She would never agree to return to Tartus, or to live in any Syrian city other than Damascus. But when there is a job vacancy I can fill, I will return to Tartus because I have gotten sick of life in the capital. My life here has gotten boring, and I have neither family here nor even a comfortable home. Sometimes a week passes without my talking to a woman, except perhaps a formal conversation with a married colleague. I hate the loneliness and emptiness in Yabrud and Damascus. If it weren't for Zuhayr, I would suffocate. I am afraid I have become a burden on Zuhayr; every week he is bound to me and to my plans. Perhaps he has his own plans or business to take care of, especially on Thursday evenings. I must stop calling him every Thursday. I could vary my weekly travels and go one week to Damascus, one week to Homs, one week to Aleppo…"

"Hello, Yusuf!" A voice drew him away from his thoughts, and before he knew who was speaking he answered hello. When he turned to see who it was, he saw Ahmad Abbud.

"Hello there, Ahmad. What brings you to Damascus?"

"I've been called up. What about you? Didn't they call you

up? We did our service together, your unit—"

Yusuf was surprised at first, but then he remembered the tension in the general political climate and the circumstances in Lebanon. His own personal situation passed through his mind again, and he said, "I hope so. A chance to change my surroundings. I did my military service in Tartus; I will return there."

"You don't know where they will send you off to?" Ahmad Abbud asked, his discomfort showing.

"No, I served in the coastal artillery unit. But why did they call you up now?" Ahmad was surprised at Yusuf's question. He knew that Yusuf could not be so unaware of the political situation and current tensions. The two of them were students together at the public high school of Tartus. In those days, Yusuf was extremely politically active. Ahmad was one of the people who had bought the communist newspaper *Al-Sha'ab* from Yusuf and knew that he continued to be politically committed.

"It seems as though you have abandoned your political interests, Yusuf," Ahmad said. "Are you bored with politics and distributing newspapers? Haven't you heard the news about Lebanon? War is on our doorstep!"

Ahmad wanted Yusuf to remember the past. Yusuf smiled. "Man, so they have their trivial problems with clay pots here in Syria. What business is it of ours?" Yusuf answered. Yusuf wanted to make Ahmad remember Ahmad's own minimal interest in politics, to remind him that he had never been politically inclined. Ahmad was the one who had wanted to go and continue his studies in America after high school, leaving this damned country and all its petty problems. "Those petty problems with clay pots are none of our business," Yusuf always used to joke sarcastically, referring to the popular Syrian saying about how one should not get involved in other people's problems.

Ahmad had not caught the sarcastic and slightly malicious tone of Yusuf's answer; perhaps he did not remember how Yusuf used to talk. In reality, Ahmad had not gone to America and had not continued his studies, but had instead opened a business. "But they're making their problems our business," he replied angrily. "I closed the shop on account of these call-ups. Do you know—"

Yusuf interrupted, "I don't have a business or money, so let the government put me where it wants. I am a civil servant. It makes no difference whether I work in the military or as a teacher." Yusuf wanted to remind Ahmad of how scornfully Ahmad had treated him when he had dropped by Ahmad's place in Tartus. Ahmad had made fun of him then for being a lowly government employee with no money.

But now here was Ahmad trying to make Yusuf feel that they shared the same misfortune, by responding with a clever allusion to the same joke: "It's more serious this time because their problems no longer involve just clay pots but missiles," Ahmad said.

Finally, when Yusuf could no longer keep his poker face, he reminded Ahmad, "You're right. I would have said that fifteen years ago too. But you did not start to differentiate between clay pots and missiles until your business started to boom. You—"

Astonished, Ahmad was jolted awake. He remembered every fight, disagreement, and conversation he had had with Yusuf and every sardonic comment Yusuf had ever made. He even remembered Yusuf's sarcastic debating style and said, laughing, "You're still a clever one. I bet you know everything, even whether there will be a war or not."

Yusuf

Yusuf left the Kindi Theater—the movie was good this week—and walked to the Nuri Bookstore. He looked at the books and did not see anything new. He figured this was because the highway to Lebanon was blocked and the situation increasingly tense—everything seemed tense. No one was interested in books, and people talked of nothing but the situation in Lebanon, the Beqa'a valley, and the missile crisis. Would Syria pull its forces out of Lebanon? Would Israel bomb the base? Yusuf was convinced that Israel would not attack. He knew that would be the focus of his conversation later with Zuhayr, who believed that they would.

Yusuf remembered that he had wanted to go to Umm Muhsin's house because perhaps the chief sergeant would have some news. "I will be so preoccupied with talking to Dallal I will forget about the missiles. I will keep busy avoiding her attacks and launching my own," he whispered under his breath to himself. After he bought a philosophy book on the Age of Enlightenment, he left the bookstore and walked toward Victoria Bridge. At the station he got in a *servees*, thinking of Dallal.

He got off at the Shaykh Sa'ad stop, walked to the chief sergeant's house, and knocked on the door. Dallal opened it and greeted him with a smile. "Welcome, Ustaz Yusuf. Hello and welcome. You have a new book, I'm sure."

Yusuf tried to seem formal so that he would perhaps be able to hide his eyes and his beating heart. "Good evening to you, Aniseh Dallal."

Dallal realized that Yusuf was speaking very formally and she decided to play the same game. She remained standing at the door looking at his face as though she were asking "Yes?" without saying "Come in." He felt ill at ease. "Is your father home?"

Smiling, she teased him again. "And if he's not here, won't you honor us with your presence? Please come in, do come in." Standing a little away from the door to make room for Yusuf as he entered, Dallal said to herself, "Our friend is either uneasy or annoyed by the intensity of our discussion and disagreement last week. Perhaps he's trying to cover it up."

Abu Muhsin's house was old and cramped. There were two bedrooms with a spacious hall separating them. The mother and father slept in one bedroom and Dallal and little Ali slept in the other. Muhammad slept on the couch in the main hall that was used as both a sitting room and a room to receive guests, which the house always seemed to be filled with—guests from the village, neighbors, Abu Muhsin's friends, Muhammad's classmates, and Dallal's friends, both male and female. Dallal used to say that one of the reasons she stayed out of the house all day was because it was so cramped and crowded. She used to joke that people should remain at home at least one evening per week, and she chose Thursday night—the night when most people go out since Friday is the weekend.

When Yusuf entered the main room, however, he noticed that it was arranged differently, that there were new covers on the furniture and a bouquet of flowers on the television set. To mask his surprise and uneasiness, he turned the conversation to the flowers.

"Beautiful flowers. They must have been chosen by Aniseh Dallal," he said. He could see that Dallal had noticed that he was ill at ease and wanted to prove that he was not uncomfortable.

"Thank you for the nice compliment," she said and snickered. The sound of the mother and father leaving their room interrupted Dallal and Yusuf.

"Welcome! How are you?" Umm Muhsin said warmly to Yusuf.

"Welcome, how are you? Why didn't you come for lunch today? Didn't Dallal invite you last week? I'm sorry, I was on duty and couldn't see you—come in!" Abu Muhsin said.

"I went to see a movie this afternoon," Yusuf replied, to give Dallal's father an excuse for not coming in the afternoon. He was actually directing his words at Dallal whom he knew followed the cinema, certain that she would ask him about the film. He wanted a way to start talking to her despite knowing that they would certainly wind up disagreeing about something.

"What film did you see?" Dallal asked.

"*The Cop*. A good film... excellent. The hero—"

"I know it, I saw it last year at the cinema club. It's a silly film." Yusuf realized that she wanted to annoy him and that she said the movie was silly only because he described it as "excellent." So he decided to fire one of his missiles back at her.

"You're right, it is silly," he said to her in a tone that meant, "I know that if I had told you that it's a silly film, you would have said, 'No, it's an excellent film.'"

Dallal did not give in though. "It's an average film about police life."

"That's what's great about the film—it shows how a normal man becomes a destructive robot." Yusuf made clear his desire to have a serious discussion with Dallal, but she bit her lip.

"It shows us a scene, one that we see every day. We see—"

Because he wanted to talk to Yusuf, Dallal's father cut her

off. "How are you, Ustaz Yusuf? How are you liking Yabrud?"

Smiling, Yusuf turned to Abu Muhsin. "Yabrud's a nice town, but life there—it's limited. There's nowhere to go except on a walk around the orchards and fields."

Umm Muhsin interrupted, "Yabrud is nearby, in less than one hour you can be in Damascus. Rent yourself a room here and go in the morning—"

Dallal broke in brusquely. "And who can find a cheap room to rent in Damascus? I would—" She wanted to say, "I would rent a room myself," but did not dare.

Abu Muhsin continued talking, "Yabrud has fields and cultivated orchards of fruit trees full of cherries and pears. My colleague Chief Sergeant Abu Nabil has a cherry orchard where he spends all of his time outside the camp."

"The life of solitude and emptiness is difficult. I cook when I am tired of restaurant food, I do laundry, and I—"

As Yusuf continued speaking, Umm Muhsin felt moved to say, "You are just like my son. Oh, Yusuf. We are family. We have a European, automatic washing machine. Bring me your clothes each week. I am like your mother, you—"

Dallal interrupted, "What's so hard for him? He or any other man? Let them do laundry. Let them cook! Let them—"

To pester her, Yusuf interrupted. "And you women, your highnesses, all go to movies and the hairdresser and the—"

This time she cut him off sharply as though she wanted a new battle. "Oh, no. We go to factories and schools and offices."

This time, Yusuf noticed how strained and forced she seemed in using her mock indignation to catch him off guard. She had known, however, even before she had stated her opinion that he would agree with it, and she wanted to give him the chance to express another opinion so that she could attack him. He understood what she was doing, and so, in order to torment her a bit more, he decided to take the bait, mocking her by imitating her tone of voice. "When we men stay home, we do laundry, cook, and clean so that you women will return home from the factories, schools, and offices and find dinner on the table. What's the use? Should we simply reverse the roles? We men will stay home and we will—"

"You will go to hell."

Yusuf was stunned that she had spoken so strongly. Dallal stopped after she uttered these words, retreating in regret. She tried to cover up her rudeness by returning to the subject that had prompted her to speak her mind in the first place, as though she were trying to complete her thought.

"Frankly, my opinion is that all men are reactionaries." What she wanted to say was "contemptible," but she held herself back. "They discuss progressive ideas in cafés, books, and other places and with women whom they want to seduce. As for 'their' women—their mothers, wives, and sisters—they exercise the most disgusting type of reactionary behavior. All Arab men are like this. All."

The sharpness of her voice rose in a crescendo. For a brief moment, Yusuf felt that she was referring to him personally and wanted to humiliate him.

"Thank God I don't have a wife, and my mother and sister are back in the village!" Yusuf hoped a joke would ease the tension.

Umm Muhsin thought this a suitable time to change the subject. "Dallal, Ali is late, where is he?"

"At the neighbor's," Dallal said sullenly.

Yusuf's joke had achieved the opposite result. Dallal felt that he was acting superior to her, being sarcastic at her expense. "That is exactly how Middle Eastern men always manage to avoid serious discussions. With laughter and sarcasm. Middle Eastern men are all like this. European men don't abuse women, they—"

"Change the subject, Dallal," her father said. He then laughed, trying to mediate between Dallal and Yusuf. "Besides, you can't say anything about Yusuf in terms of his progressiveness." After saying this with a smile, the father turned to Yusuf hoping to change the topic of conversation.

"What's the latest political news Ustaz Yusuf?" Her father insisted on addressing Yusuf with the polite title Ustaz—not to put a barrier between them, but to make Dallal understand that he respected Yusuf, and that she should be more careful how she talked to him.

"News? You have the news in the army, Abu Muhsin. You guys in the military have everything in your hands."

"The military are our rulers," Dallal interrupted jokingly, unaware that she was expressing her opinion by repeating something Yusuf had said to her the previous week almost word-for-word.

The chief sergeant clarified his question. "I mean, will a war break out or not?"

"The real answer is with the higher leadership," Yusuf said.

"May evil stay far away from us. *Inshallah* nothing will happen," Umm Muhsin said.

"Our English teacher at the university said there is going to be a full-scale war this summer," Dallal interjected.

Yusuf was surprised at whose words she was quoting and taking seriously, but then remembered that last week she had talked about her English drama professor and how she and her friends had visited him at his house. Like any villager, Yusuf was fearful and distrustful of foreigners, especially non-Arabs. "Is our brother the professor teaching you drama or giving political and military prophecies?" Yusuf felt that the irony in his voice had upset her and had provoked her again after she had started to calm down. He retreated. "You told me that this professor is a kind man. How is he doing?"

Dallal did not miss what was behind this seemingly-innocent withdrawal from his sarcastic commentary. His question may have had a serious accusation behind it or may have been simply random. She had come to know his style of covering up his retreats with jokes that were more biting than his serious attacks.

She defended herself, and to rouse his anger she mocked him, "He would like to bow down before you and kiss your hand." Then she changed her tone, becoming superior and serious. "He is a good professor and is understanding. Imagine, he is the only professor who invites students to his house. Tomorrow is Friday, and he is going to take us to Bosra in his car."

Yusuf felt something tugging at his heart and asked himself, "Am I jealous?" But then he told himself, "What's the use of being jealous? What is there between me and her that I should be jealous? Damn her, let her come and go and do what she wants, when she wants."

After realizing how seriously her words had affected Yusuf, Dallal resumed, "Can you imagine an Arab professor doing that? He invites us to tea in his house and he takes us in his car to show us archaeological sites and ancient ruins. He knows the Old City of Damascus better than we do. Even we—"

"Do these tourist guides come here simply for God's sake? Is it free of charge? They take us in their cars, they invite us to their fancy houses 'for the sake of history' and to show us the truth—" Yusuf felt that his getting so worked up was embarrassing and unwarranted, especially his terse, nasty tone. He stopped in mid-sentence and changed the rhythm of his speech, taking refuge in his usual derisive camouflage. "Could I have a place with your group or are your trips for British only?" He knew that he had fallen back on his standard ironic tone despite himself, and he thought, "Damn it! I guess I am just like this and it's hard to change." He thought of another answer that seemed more polite and less tense, but then he noticed that Dallal's mother was no longer there. "Where is Umm Muhsin?" he asked.

"She went to the neighbor's to pick up Ali; he's late," Dallal said. She noticed the way Yusuf changed the subject.

"I have a date with a friend, and I'm late too. The appointment is at nine." Yusuf was pleased at the chance to talk about Ali's lateness, so as to give him a reason to leave.

"Stay, sit down. Let's have dinner together!" Dallal's father extended a sincere invitation to Yusuf.

"Thank you, but I'm afraid I might be late to meet my friend," he said.

"Come visit us next week!" Abu Muhsin said. Then he suggested that Yusuf come to Damascus whenever he was bored—he did not only have to come on Thursdays.

In the tone of someone who has vanquished the enemy, Dallal offered, "Come next Thursday. I will introduce you to the English professor. We are going to meet at three-thirty in front of the Kindi Theater. We'll see the movie and then go have coffee somewhere." She was quiet, and then the rest of her invitation came out halfway between sarcasm and provocation. "We'll be waiting for you—Ustaz Yusuf."

Zuhayr

"Y ou're late! Where have you been? Of course the one who is with his lovers forgets his friends… God, I've missed you," Zuhayr Qawasmi said, welcoming his friend. Yusuf felt the sincerity of Zuhayr's emotions and the deep feeling of friendship he had for him. Zuhayr lived by himself, not with his family, though they also lived in Damascus. Yusuf had met him when they were both students at the University of Damascus. At that time, Yusuf only came into Damascus to take exams. During the winters he taught in the countryside in Jezira. Zuhayr was working in the courthouse, studying, reading novels, and harboring aspirations of becoming a novelist sometime in the future. When he failed to become a novelist, he became a lazy journalist for one of the official state newspapers *Teshreen*. But he had retained his ambition to become a novelist, as well as his observational skills and talent for both speaking and answering questions, which he now used to joke with words, make puns, and give surprise answers in conversations.

"I'm not late! I had a heated argument with the young lady about women and the British." Yusuf had told Zuhayr about his relative's family and about Dallal.

"So that means you're happy that you came?" Zuhayr picked up this thread of conversation. "You joker, you should have said that you were with Dallal! Why didn't you, are you afraid?"

Yusuf felt like a fox who had lead a dog to the safety of his own den. He found that the safest and most sure defense in the face of Zuhayr's sarcasm was to attack back with the same. "Do you think I was there to make decisions on matters of war and peace with the most honorable Chief Sergeant?"

Zuhayr knew Yusuf well and realized from his bitterly ironic answer that his friend was determined to hide his emotions, even from himself. "Did you convince her of your opinions in the end? Did you tame her or did she tame you? Of course I don't care about either your opinion or hers, but I do care about which one of you convinced the other. In these situations, I am the one who is convinced, I surrender—"

Yusuf realized that Zuhayr's question meant, "Did you fall in love with her?" for Zuhayr continually bragged about women. "She invited me to the movies," he said.

Zuhayr was not surprised, so to be totally honest with his friend, Yusuf said, "But she will be with her professor," trying to give his voice an ironic tone. He was silent for a moment. "The British guy."

This time, Zuhayr was surprised. "The British guy? Her English professor?"

"The Drama professor. I told you what she said about him last time. That he invites his students on picnics and to his house and—"

Zuhayr seized this idea. "And to cafeterias and restaurants, and after that to his house, and once in his house to—"

"You think only about people's ulterior motives!" Yusuf said.

Zuhayr laughed and continued, "You are the suspicious one! I know you. You told me about the British professor who invited both his male and female students to his house because you know me and you know how I think. You want me to tell you what you think deep down because you do not dare to say it. Because it hurts you to think it. You want me to be suspicious about Dallal going to his house because you are suspicious, and you want me to express your suspicions. Listen, I'm going to explain my theory to you about women who hang around with foreigners. I want to ask you what Dallal means to you."

26

Yusuf answered quickly. "No, nothing—she's not particularly special to me personally at all."

"Liar! You say 'no' in a way that I understand to mean 'yes.' You have started to talk like a silly teenage girl, my friend. You have started to fall in love with her, but you are hiding it from yourself, because you don't have the guts to tell her. You don't love her completely but you have started to fall for her, you—"

"Enough, enough. Explain your theory to me."

"Take it easy! We should have a drink first," Zuhayr said. "I wait for you to come down every Thursday so we can go out and drink together. I've really missed you; I'll treat you to dinner at the Vendôme. You came in from the countryside, and you should enjoy yourself—have a little fun! I have to entertain you, so I'm going to show you places that you will soon go to with Dallal."

"Do you think that I'm coming to your house from the stables, my sophisticated gentleman?" Yusuf asked.

"God forbid, Ustaz. But I am Damascene, and no matter how experienced you are in these matters, I am more experienced—it's in my genes. Come on, let's go! Your nerves are shot these days and I've got a lot of money. We'll drink French wine. Enjoy yourself!"

"Why don't you tell me about your theory we were talking about before?" Yusuf wished to continue the previous discussion because he was sure that Zuhayr would somehow refer subtly to Dallal.

"'There is a time for love and a time for death,' as Remarque said. I say 'There is a time for talk.' I'll tell you about it on the way. Go on, don't be afraid! We'll come back home to sleep. I've started hating staying at home, man. I'll tell you, but I hope that talking about your relative will not bother you. The way she talks about the English professor reminds me of the theory of a friend of mine. I'm saying that it's my theory too because I totally believe in it. Listen and don't interpret this conversation as being directed toward or against anyone specific. The whole matter—"

"Don't you feel that you are giving an unusually long-winded introduction?" Yusuf asked Zuhayr in order to push him to get to the point directly.

"All right, all right. The theory is really funny. It claims that there are three kinds of prostitutes. The first are the 'proletarian prostitutes.' They are the cheapest, but most honorable prostitutes. They fulfill a social need in this ridiculous society, and they live by the sweat of their brows and the working of their vaginas. Second, there are the 'intellectual prostitutes.' They work within the intellectual milieu in the name of culture, politics, and freedom. They are the most contemptible. They cost more money than the first type. They are a group of women and girls who used to be 'good girls' some time in the past, but they crave the bright lights. This and their small minds make them lose their way. They are the kind of women that writers, journalists, filmmakers, and artists exchange. They moan with ecstasy whenever there is singing; they gather in front of paintings. You see them at films, festivals, coffee shops. I tell you, they are the worst kind. No, actually they are the weakest ones, and we should pity them—"

"Oh, may God have mercy on your kind heart."

Zuhayr ignored Yusuf's sarcastic comment. "Then, there's the third type, and these are the ones we're interested in here, the reason why we started this conversation. The third kind, sir, are the 'foreign expatriate-community prostitutes,' and this kind—"

Yusuf thought that Zuhayr must still be feeling badly about his experience with Layla, the woman whom he had truly loved. He had wanted to marry her last year, but instead she married a French journalist. Now the thought of Dallal and the drama professor made Yusuf feel as if a knife were twisting in his heart. He tried not to show what he was thinking because he knew how clever Zuhayr was; he would quickly notice any change in Yusuf's tone of voice or facial expression.

Zuhayr continued. "This type is the most dangerous type. They move about in an environment of spies, pretenders, misers, peacocks, and others who have lost the capability for true love. Yusuf, brother, you know how much I love and respect you. Listen to me. I'm not smarter than you, and I despise taking on the role of teacher or master. But I know this city better than you do, and that is why I am so honest with you. I know my honesty may be hurtful—"

"Like all honesty," Yusuf remarked.

"And all truth. Yusuf, don't be offended but I am afraid that your relative Dallal is one of the third kind, or on the way there. Don't get involved, Yusuf. This girl is neither from Damascus nor from your village. Deep down, this girl has a backward mentality, she is lost."

Yusuf felt defensive and emotional. "No, no, I'm not involved with her. It's only a normal relationship. I won't get involved."

"Don't be like Antar, the great romantic hero," Zuhayr said calmly. "The more you say, the more I understand you. You can lie to yourself but you can't lie to me. You've started to feel something for this girl." Zuhayr paused. "I may be wrong in my suspicions. She may be a nice young woman. Just be careful. Who knows, Yusuf. Maybe it's just that regular disappointment with women has made me think badly of them."

From Zuhayr's sorrowful tone, Yusuf could tell that Zuhayr was thinking about Layla. He thought of asking about Layla but instead suggested, "As long as she is going to go with her friends and the British professor to a movie next Thursday, what do you think about coming with me?"

Zuhayr did not answer. He was certain that Yusuf was seeking some kind of protection and safety. He would go more for support and solidarity than out of a desire to see the movie. Whatever was keeping Yusuf together was beginning to crumble.

They had almost arrived at the entrance to the Vendôme. After they had sat down at their table, Zuhayr said, "I'll go with you. But let's change the subject. What's the latest news? Will war break out or not? Drink some wine, old man. Damn the whole world! Drink up, I've missed you, I really have."

Zuhayr

They left the Vendôme restaurant after each of them had drunk a bottle of French wine. Yusuf had fallen into a deeply depressed mood. He felt the desire to be alone and thought about how to excuse himself from sleeping at Zuhayr's house, but what would Zuhayr think? This would come as a surprise. Yusuf had been sleeping over at Zuhayr's regularly for two years; in fact, he almost had his own room at Zuhayr's place with some of his books and clothes. Yusuf could not think of a better way than telling the truth directly, "Zuhayr, you understand me. Forgive me for not going back with you, but I really want to be by myself, to walk in the streets alone."

Zuhayr was surprised. At first, he thought that Yusuf was upset about the way he had discussed Dallal, but then he rejected this idea because he knew that Yusuf trusted him. He said to himself that it must be the wine. But Yusuf was not usually affected by this amount of wine, and this was not the first time that they had gone out drinking together. Zuhayr spoke kindly. "Go ahead, leave out all the philosophizing. I'm not going to let you drink anymore after tonight! You are used to the—"

"Zuhayr, I'll come home in an hour if my mental state improves." Yusuf thought that Zuhayr was being so gentle with him because he thought him drunk. He felt a true brotherly love for Zuhayr, mixed with sorrow. "But I need to be alone for a while."

It flashed through Zuhayr's mind that Yusuf was thinking about Dallal, that he was daydreaming and spacing out during the political conversation in the restaurant because he was thinking about something else—Dallal. He thought to himself that he should not have joked about the prostitution theory. "I definitely hurt Yusuf's feelings, I wouldn't have thought that he would fall in love so quickly and so easily." Zuhayr's analysis was that young men from the country were overly emotional and honest about their feelings. No matter how rational they seemed, they fell in love quickly, and until they had matured, they were unable to hide it. It was better to let Yusuf do what he wanted.

"Do I need to tell you that my house is your house?" Zuhayr's voice held a mixture of love and pity. "You can come and go whenever you want. You have the keys."

He walked toward his house in the Mezra'a district, remembering a similar love story that he himself had lived through. It was as though Yusuf had reopened an old wound that Zuhayr had thought was already healed. He would have liked to be with Yusuf. He wished that he could have convinced him to stay with him so they could talk about Layla again. Layla had returned to live in his imagination once again. As he reached the beginning of Salhiyyeh Street, he asked himself why he had not married Layla. Why did he let her marry a French guy and go with him to France? He remembered that he had always tried to seem as though he did not care about her or his emotions when he was with her. She tried to play his game—she let him know that she did not care about him either, or indeed about anything in her life in Syria, and that she would marry a Frenchman because life in Damascus was unbearable. Now, he finally realized that he had loved her, he still loved her, and would continue to love her. He knew now for certain that she had loved him, that she continued to love him, and that she did not leave with the Frenchman for any reason other than to run away from him. She had fled after exploding in his face one day, screaming, "I love you and you are cruel. You are cold to me just so that you can humiliate me. No, no—I won't give you the pleasure! I'm the one who will humiliate you. I will make you miss me forever. Who do you think you are?"

He remembered how he used to call out to her jokingly, "Come here, you little bitch." And how she would answer him, "Yes, my cruel and honorable master"—even when they used to kiss each other. He remembered how much she used to like Yusuf and how she used to talk to him about her love for Zuhayr. Meanwhile, he would be having the same conversation with Yusuf. He remembered how he and Layla used to play games, pretend to meet coincidentally.

After deciding not to go home but rather to walk around the streets alone, like Yusuf, he drew near Jahiz Park. He passed by the Dar Café and remembered that he used to go there on dates with Layla. He made a joke to himself, saying that subconsciously he must have come here in order to stand at the abandoned campsite like the great hero always does in pre-Islamic poetry after his beloved has moved away. He thought about Yusuf and wondered where he had gone. He thought to himself that Yusuf definitely loved Dallal, and that he might have gotten upset at the mention of "foreign expatriate-community prostitutes." He knew that a man who has fallen in love with a woman does not want to have bad thoughts about her. He thought to himself, "I'll meet this Dallal next week." He went into the deserted café and ordered a cup of coffee, wishing that Yusuf were with him, wishing that Layla were there, wishing that a woman he loved were there now drinking a cup of coffee with him.

He thought about the young women he knew. He decided that they were the second type, the "intellectual prostitutes."

He thought about his many interconnected relationships and how easily he could be with one of the young women he knew now. He recalled Fatin, Jacqueline, Henaa, and Reem and felt something like the taste of ashes rise in his throat. He ordered a bottle of wine. Layla returned to take hold of his thoughts. He remembered her inviting him to France for a two-week stay at her house with her and her husband, Jean-Claude Chrétien. He thought about her last visit to Damascus—how she had talked about her happy life with Jean-Claude, and how at the time he felt that her talk of happiness was simply to provoke him. He was sure that she was unfaithful in her Parisian life. "It was one of the few times I stopped treating her badly and I pretended that I believed her so that I wouldn't hurt her. I truly wish her well, although I know it is impossible for her to be happy." Zuhayr knew that Layla was lying to him so that he would not rub it in that she was unhappy. He even knew that she was thinking about divorce, but she was not brave enough to announce her failure—at least in front of him. He drank one last sip of coffee and felt sleepy.

He got up and walked toward his house. Damascus was so beautiful late at night! He felt a strong attachment to these streets. He walked slowly, picking a branch of jasmine and smelling it. He recalled walking with Layla on these streets, how she used to pick the jasmine and give it to him, joking, "You take it, even though you don't deserve it." Then she would take it back. "Don't listen to me, you deserve jasmine and even more." He wished to himself that he would accidentally run into Yusuf. He knew that like him Yusuf was wandering the streets. He kept feeling like talking about Layla. Remembering his theory about the three types of prostitutes, he thought, "I am a big-mouth and maybe even a hateful person." Possibly Yusuf might have thought that he was referring to Layla and her marriage to the Frenchman when he was talking about the trio of prostitutes. But Yusuf had not confronted him with this opinion out of respect for his feelings.

Again, he felt that he wanted to find Yusuf and confess that he still loved Layla. Maybe when he got home he would find that Yusuf had gotten there before him. "Here's Yusuf starting the same story that I finished one year ago," he whispered to himself. "No one can help anyone else in these situations. Each person must pluck out the thorn stuck in his side with his own hands."

He remembered all the advice Yusuf had given him, how much he had comforted him, and that it did not change anything. No one can teach anyone anything in this life. He got home and Yusuf was not there as he had hoped and half-expected. He said aloud, joking with Yusuf as though he were standing right in front of him, "My friend, you are going to be walking in the streets until morning when you will get a cup of coffee in Rawda!"

Like a comedian who uses very formal Arabic to make the crowd laugh, he raised his voice to tease his friend whom he was still joking around with, but realized that he was stuck because there were no more jokes left to make. As he turned out the lights to go to sleep Zuhayr announced to the imaginary Yusuf, "May God forgive your errors—you who forgive the errors of others."

Fawziya

Fawziya Sabbagh was a 26-year-old woman. In her first year at college, she fell in love with a classmate in the English literature department. Since Sami was from another sect, it was a stormy and scandalous love affair, but it ended in a surprise marriage in her second year of university. By the end of the third academic year, she had become a divorced woman with a child. She did not register for classes for three years and kept busy giving private lessons and raising her child until this year, when she returned to third-year classes to complete some required courses. It was there, in the evening classes, that she met Dallal Muhammad. After meeting two or three times, they became fast friends. Soon afterward, Dallal told Fawziya about available positions for teachers in the secondary school in Dariya and wrote her a recommendation.

Fawziya was a disappointed woman. Her tempestuous love affair with Sami caused her to have an attitude of general disrespect for men, coupled with a longing for some certain, but unknown, man. Fawziya lived with her divorced mother and her son, Ra'id. She told Dallal that the curse of divorce was chasing her family. She and her mother dealt with things just as one might expect two destroyed women in solidarity with each other would. They were two women betrayed by both men and time, and who persevered, waiting for a certain something, a certain man, a certain incident. This is why they spent so much time reading coffee cups and interpreting dreams.

Sometimes, when the feelings of emptiness became overwhelming, they threw cocktail parties, hosted luncheons or soirées with dancing—all in the hope that these gatherings would perhaps lessen the loneliness. They invited male and female friends, both the mother's—Faiza—and Fawziya's. They divided their attention equally among all the guests. From time to time, they might let a word of disrespect for men, especially Middle Eastern men, slip out, but they both worked hard throwing parties, making the invitations, receiving guests, and seeing men in dreams and coffee cups. They had long ago closed the door on this hope and now would only open it halfway, but the young men who spent evenings with them at their parties could sense the opening in the once-locked doorway. Of course, the type of men and families that Faiza invited to her house would not think about exploiting the loneliness of two divorced and lonely women who maintained chaste relationships with respectable people at the same time that they harbored a hidden passion for men.

It was into this scene that Dallal entered. As time passed, she grew to love Faiza, and she even began to find the Middle Eastern femininity within herself that she had hidden behind the mask of her education and liberation. In the past, she had been contemptuous about reading coffee cups and interpreting dreams. But now she stopped by at Fawziya's from time to time, using the excuse that she missed her and Ra'id or that she was simply passing through the neighborhood, when actually she was coming to drink coffee and to face her fears with Sitt Faiza. With time, Dallal started to tell Faiza about her dreams, but in front of Yusuf, her friends, and her classmates, she continued to attack the reading of coffee cups and the interpretation of dreams, ridiculing "these absurd Middle Eastern practices" as she described them. Today she came to visit Sitt Faiza to tell her a dream she had had the night before.

Dallal stopped by Fawziya's house without warning that she was coming beforehand and did not find Fawziya at home. She pretended that she had been passing through the neighborhood and that she simply felt like visiting Sitt Faiza and Ra'id. But Faiza understood what Dallal was like and what she was after. The moment Dallal entered the house, Faiza could tell by how she was talking that Dallal had come to ask her for advice and to recount her dreams. What do young women Dallal's age dream about? What do they search for in coffee cups? Faiza understood these things well.

"Welcome Dallal, daughter. You know that I love you like Fawziya. Do you only visit us when you are passing through the neighborhood?"

Faiza said this pretending that she was scolding Dallal, but the tone of her voice revealed that she knew that her guest had come on purpose. Dallal realized that Faiza had found her out and that she suspected the truth of why she had come. "No, no—I came especially for you. How could it be otherwise?" she said.

"And you are always welcome here. This house is your house, and you should feel that I am like your mother," Faiza said to make Dallal feel that she was in a safe and friendly environment. "I'm going to prepare coffee for you."

She said this so as not to embarrass Dallal, since Faiza had come to understand this young woman and knew that she wanted her to read her coffee cup though she would outwardly display a lack of interest and even protest against it. She added, "I'm going to read your cup." Then she abandoned all formality and added with a smile, "Maybe we'll find you a husband."

"All the young men are blind these days. When will a man

with a blind heart find me?" Dallal asked jokingly.

"That is not the problem my dear—you are beautiful," Faiza said. "The question is where will we find you one with two open eyes and an open heart? Men—"

They heard the sound of a key turning in the door. Fawziya walked in with Ra'id. Dallal hurried over toward him and picked him up, kissing and playing with him. She took some candy out of her purse and gave it to Ra'id. "My darling Ra'id—will you come home with me?"

"Go ahead! Take him." It was obvious that this three-year-old child liked spending time outside the house and that the hour he had spent in the public park with his mother was not enough. "Sit down and be quiet," Fawziya ordered him.

Making fun of herself as well as the boy, Dallal interjected, "He's just like me. He doesn't like to stay home—tomorrow *I'll* take him to the park!"

"Make some coffee for us, Fawziya. Ra'id, come over here by me," Faiza said, turning to the boy and adding, "If only children would stay children! Men are so nice when they are young. It's when they grow up that they get worse and especially—"

"Especially after they get married," Dallal said, touching on what she knew was a sensitive topic for Faiza and Fawziya. Trying to show that she had a distinct personality independent of her mother's, Fawziya said, "No, some of them are sweet and nice." Winking at Dallal, she added, "Dr. Morton White is a man, and he's cute! I'll go and make the coffee."

They drank the coffee and talked about the gathering the week before at Faiza's house when Fawziya had invited Dr. Morton White. Fawziya said to Dallal, "Our house is your house. If your house is ever crowded you should always consider this your home."

Faiza reached out her hand to Dallal. "Give me your cup. Or don't you want me to see your cup?" Faiza wanted to discover Dallal's true intentions, perhaps even to force her to make her wishes clear.

"As you like," answered Dallal, leaving the matter up in the air as she always did when someone was trying to discover her true motives.

Fawziya jumped into the conversation, encouraging Dallal. "No, she wants to. Ra'id come here, give me the cup, would you."

Dallal held her cup out in her hand and Faiza noticed her trembling. Faiza stared at the cup and turned it upside down. Then she turned it around in circles. A minute of ponderous silence passed. Dallal did not know how the words crossed her lips, but before Faiza could speak she said, "Sitt Faiza, I had a strange dream."

Faiza realized that Dallal could hold back no longer and that her apparent composure had given way, so she let her speak. Another minute of silence stretched out before them. Dallal began, "I saw someone, no, no, I should tell the truth, I should not hide anything from you—I saw our professor."

Dallal turned to Fawziya in order to see her reaction to what she had said and then turned her glance to the wall, like someone trying to escape from the gaze of other people. She continued, "Professor, Professor Morton White, I saw him hugging me, kissing me, and I was submitting, and all of a sudden I pushed him away from me. I screamed, 'Go away, leave me alone you disgusting man!' He was smiling, and I saw myself jump on him and then hug him. I pushed him away a second time and screamed, 'You're despicable!' Then I woke up. It's strange, I do not feel anything special for him. I simply respect him as a professor, and as an educated and truly liberated man—a progressive man."

Holding herself back, Dallal continued praising the professor and talking seriously. But then she said sarcastically, "They are silly dreams." And then, as if begging to be reassured about something she was uncertain of, "Aren't they?"

"Let's see what the coffee cup says..." Faiza said.

Layla

It was Thursday afternoon. Zuhayr Qawasmi was waiting at home for Yusuf, so when the phone rang he was sure it would be Yusuf on the other end. But the caller was Layla. At first, he thought she was calling from Paris to ask him for a favor, as she often did—to chase after some of her documents or to send something she needed. But instead she asked him if he could meet her.

Zuhayr was unsure of what to do. He had a date to meet Yusuf at the cinema and he felt that Yusuf really needed him this time. Besides, he had a secret desire to meet Dallal and Morton White, maybe just to test out how true his theory was.

But politeness dictated that he must ask after Jean-Claude. Layla said that he would be with her, and that he was the one responsible for them coming. Zuhayr felt once again that she was trying to convince him that she was happy, and that her relationship with her husband was improving. She said that they would stay in Damascus for one week. Since Jean-Claude was a journalist, he always surfaced when there was tension in the region.

Zuhayr teased her, reminding her of their previous conversations by saying that it was natural Jean-Claude should be in the line of fire. She understood what he was implying and responded with a touch of malice. "You *are* the line of fire, most honorable and nasty sir."

He asked if they could postpone their meeting until the next day because he was very busy that afternoon and most likely in the evening as well. "As compensation, I'd like to invite the two of you to a big Friday lunch in Dumar tomorrow and Yusuf will come with us," he said.

Layla asked after Yusuf and Zuhayr told her that Yusuf was managing to get by. He thought about Yusuf for a moment. "But his defenses are starting to crumble."

They made the appointment for the next day and said good-bye. Zuhayr replaced the phone. "These journalists, they're all spies, they come and… this means the situation is really tense. War will break out—definitely."

At three o'clock, Yusuf rang the bell. The moment Zuhayr saw Yusuf he could sense that he was nervous but trying hard to hide it. Zuhayr pretended that he had forgotten about the invitation to the movie. "Time moves slowly and heavily in the afternoon. What is a man to do? Sleep? Roam the streets?"

Yusuf picked up on Zuhayr's feigned forgetfulness about their date, and decided that he would attack his friend before he could continue with his barbs. "You could come with me and my friends to the Kindi Theater. We are going to see *Sacco and Vanzetti*. Let's go—it's rude to make them wait at the door for us."

Zuhayr smiled, knowing that Yusuf could maintain a cold and distant composure no matter how nervous or worried he was. "Yusuf, I wish I could go with you, but Layla and her husband are in town. She called me and we—"

"Layla's in town?" Yusuf seemed astonished.

"You know the cinema is always here and the film was shown before. Layla has only a few days in Damascus, and then she will—"

This time, Yusuf was embarrassed. He felt that it was small of him to insist that Zuhayr accompany him to the cinema when he knew about Zuhayr's feelings for Layla. But he did feel that he really needed Zuhayr beside him. By default, he chose an embarrassing silence and turned his face toward the wall so that Zuhayr would not be able to read any expression.

Zuhayr realized that he had backed Yusuf into a corner and that he had had enough, so he said, "Come on, let's go— Layla's married! Maybe there will be some pretty young women with Dallal."

Yusuf had worked out that Zuhayr would go with him and was simply playing with him. He decided to keep the game alive by throwing the ball back into Zuhayr's court saying, "No, if Layla's in town and you promised her... Anyway, it's better if I go alone." Yusuf was sure that Zuhayr would never let him down; he knew what a good friend Zuhayr was to him. But he also knew that Zuhayr liked to play jokes on him. He had acquired this style of interacting with people from working at the newspaper. Zuhayr looked at Yusuf's face and then burst out laughing, "Oh, come on old man! You are better than the best woman." He was quiet for a moment, then he laughed. "Of the third kind, of course."

They arrived at the Kindi Theater at three-thirty. A few minutes later, a car full of people pulled up. Yusuf realized Dallal was in it and that the driver was Morton White. Dallal hurried over to start the introductions to make the others feel that she was in charge of the formalities. "Dr. Morton White, Mrs. Fawziya Sabbagh, Miss Lamis al-Muradi, Ahmad Abd al-Sitar, and Marwan al-Muhayri." She turned to Yusuf and continued, "Ustaz Yusuf." She was then quiet, leaving Yusuf to introduce his friend. He started, "Zuhayr," but taking note of the formal atmosphere added, "Ustaz Zuhayr Qawasmi... my friend."

"I have enough tickets for everyone," Dallal said. She walked ahead of them toward the door where the ticket-taker was standing, as though she wanted to give everyone the impression that she knew him better than they did because she frequented this theater.

Yusuf was thinking about the seating arrangement. Where would Dallal sit—beside the Englishman or beside him? In the end, she sat between Lamis and Fawziya, letting the other five people sit beside each other.

Zuhayr thought about how Yusuf must be feeling. This was a ridiculous situation created by an inexperienced and unsophisticated girl to hide her feelings for a specific man. Meanwhile, Yusuf explained it to himself as Dallal being confused or trying to appear serious when she attended a movie. Maybe she wanted to convey this impression to him so that he would not change his opinion of her.

Morton White

Yusuf left the film without understanding anything; he had only seen pictures following each other without being able to connect them. He had been thinking for a week about the ambiguous relationship between himself and Dallal. He questioned how he felt about being with her and these other people with whom he did not feel comfortable. He felt suspicious of the student-teacher relationship between Dallal and Morton White. Yusuf did not like the way the professor looked; he especially disliked his blond beard. All of this made him tired, seeing one thing and thinking about something else. He blamed himself for getting himself into a situation that he thought he had left behind long ago. He would say good-bye to Dallal at the door to the theater and go to a restaurant with Zuhayr. Maybe they could then try to call Layla and invite her and Jean-Claude to dinner.

"I'm sorry Aniseh Dallal, I apologize but I have to leave," he said, trying to direct his words at Dallal as they were walking out. "Thank you for the invitation." Or perhaps he wanted to apologize in his own way, and by not paying attention to the others make Dallal understand that he was not comfortable in these surroundings with her friends, both male and female, and especially with the British professor.

"No, there is a surprise," said Morton White in an Arabic that showed he was trying to imitate the local dialect. He then went silent and stared at Dallal. She smiled and said to Yusuf and Zuhayr, "Stay with us."

"You are invited to my house for a small celebration," Morton White said. He stood quietly staring with a smile at

Dallal. "Don't they know what the occasion is?"

"No, I did not tell them," Dallal answered with a laugh. "It's not my idea, but the professor insisted on a celebration when he found out. He insisted on a British-style tea party—"

Morton White took over the conversation once again, speaking in stilted Arabic. "Dallal shy, like all girls in your country. She embarrassed to say that today her birthday... come on, get in the car."

Yusuf tried to refuse, but Zuhayr was busy laughing with Fawziya. He knew that Zuhayr would welcome spending the evening with these women, caring nothing about either Dallal's birthday or Morton White's personality. Courtesy made it extremely difficult to object in this situation, so Yusuf said politely, "I must ask my friend. Zuhayr, what do you say?"

"About what?" answered Zuhayr, with a laugh.

Yusuf muttered under his breath, "The bastard knows what the deal is and he's pretending he doesn't." Gritting his teeth, Yusuf said, "Today is Aniseh Dallal's birthday." Yusuf was going to continue, "and she invited us to her party," but something inside him made him say, "and Dr. Morton White has invited us to celebrate at his house."

Dallal realized that Yusuf had launched one of his attacks in her direction, but she ignored it and acted busy by whispering in Lamis al-Muradi's ear. The other two men were waiting without saying a word. Dallal turned to Fawziya, "Did you tell your mother so she will not worry if we are late?"

Zuhayr said in a boisterous voice, "I am always ready for a celebration—anywhere, any time!"

"The problem of getting there remains," Dallal said.

"The place is just nearby in Abu Rummaneh, can you follow us?" Morton White asked while the group moved toward the car. Yusuf noticed that Dallal opened the front passenger door in a way that showed she was used to it and as though it were her right to sit in the front seat beside Morton White. When they reached the house, Morton White got out of the car and said, "Go ahead into the house before me, I forgot to get one little thing... I'll just go get it. Here, Dallal take the key."

They went into the house with Dallal going first. Yusuf did not understand the silence and shyness of the other two young men. Meanwhile Zuhayr was saying to himself, "Two young, naïve male students, invited here for camouflage, but Fawziya is beautiful." As for Lamis al-Muradi, she was trying to exchange sporadic words with Yusuf who was observing Dallal's movement about the house. He noticed that Dallal knew the house well and also that the table had been prepared ahead of time. He also noticed that there was more than just tea but a variety of Syrian dishes as well. He was certain that Dallal had prepared them. He was even more certain when he saw plates of *shanglish* and *tabbouleh*. Dallal opened the refrigerator and took out sliced meats, mortadella, and fruit. Yusuf's eyes met Zuhayr's over the dish of *shanglish*.

Morton White came into the room. He was carrying a cake with the number 23 and "Happy Birthday" written on it in incorrect Arabic. He was also carrying a bottle of champagne. Zuhayr whispered in Yusuf's ear, "Did they invite us for tea or champagne?"

Yusuf's dark and ironic humor was sparked. He whispered, "Our ears must have heard wrong. We are getting old and can no longer distinguish."

"No, you are backward, you don't distinguish between—" Zuhayr began.

Dallal noticed the whispering and knew that they were definitely talking about her. "Private conversations are not allowed!" she called out. "Change your seats, please."

Zuhayr had started to feel like he was watching a play, and so he decided that he would act in it. He drew close to Yusuf and whispered sarcastically again, "What about touching? If that's not allowed I'm going to leave. I'll—"

He had not yet finished his whisper when he noticed Dallal looking at him angrily. He moved away from Yusuf and tried to apologize. "I'm sorry, Aniseh. I just remembered something very important that I needed to tell him and I was afraid I might forget it."

"If it's really important you won't forget it. I wouldn't forget it." Dallal answered as though she were trying to let him know that she did not believe him. Zuhayr glanced toward the two male students, still sitting silently. "We said change your seats," Dallal said.

Zuhayr got up and sat near Fawziya while Morton White passed around glasses of whiskey and wine. After everyone had taken a glass, Morton White said, "Now, let's make a toast. Here's to Aniseh Dallal's health."

Zuhayr stood up with a sweeping, theatrical movement, forcing the others to stand as well. Meanwhile, Yusuf silently rebuked himself for accepting the invitation to both the movie and the professor's house. He racked his brain for a polite way to excuse himself from the situation and leave. They drank to Dallal's health and then sat down again. Zuhayr was looking around and taking in the elegant décor of the fancy house.

Yusuf looked at Zuhayr, hoping to signal his desire to leave, but Zuhayr was occupied in a lively conversation with Fawziya while Dallal was whispering to Lamis al-Muradi and breaking her own rule about whispering. Yusuf's feeling that he was superfluous grew stronger. He looked at Zuhayr who was writing something in Fawziya's address book and was sure it was his phone number. "Zuhayr," he said.

Zuhayr turned and made a motion with his hand indicating to Yusuf that he wanted him to slow down and wait a few minutes. But Yusuf could not wait any longer. He felt that every moment he stayed he lost something. He moved toward Zuhayr and suggested that they leave right away. Zuhayr looked into Yusuf's eyes and sensed despondency so deep he could not even fathom it. Zuhayr turned to Fawziya and said, "Call me."

He then decided to help Yusuf by taking the initiative. In a happy voice, he turned to Dallal and said, "Happy Birthday, Aniseh. I have to thank Yusuf for introducing me to you. Please excuse us but we are very busy. We've got another appointment this evening. I wish you had told us sooner. Best wishes for many more happy birthdays."

Dallal was surprised and felt uncomfortable. She felt that she had lost something but she did not know what—the wall she had been leaning on, or perhaps a safety net. She felt that Yusuf's leaving was going to put her in a compromising position. She tried to keep them there but they refused. Morton White intervened in a friendly way, but Yusuf could not take it any more. He had to leave.

Zuhayr

"That Ahmad Abd al-Sitar makes me laugh, and that—what's his name?—Muhayri? They were like two puppets," Zuhayr said, wanting to talk about the evening at Morton White's house.

Yusuf had started to get hold of himself. "Madame Fawziya's rear end made you even happier, you scoundrel!" he said, laughing.

"What was even better and much funnier was your confusion, good sir. You were like a fifteen-year- old boy. You're crazy. Why didn't you stay? If not for Dallal, then why not for Lamis al-Muradi? She's a polite and beautiful young woman. We should have stayed, eaten dinner, stayed up late together and—"

"You're right." Yusuf said to cut Zuhayr off. Yusuf knew that Zuhayr did not like those kinds of gatherings but rather was pushing him to talk about Dallal. He noticed a certain blame in his friend's eyes because he had lost control and withdrawn. Then he thought, "I must speak frankly with Zuhayr."

"Zuhayr, what do you think of Dallal?"

Yusuf was surprised to see Zuhayr's face change and take on a serious expression. "You'll definitely be shocked by my opinion of her. You think—I know that you sometimes pretend to read my mind, and you think that I immediately classified her as the third type of prostitute—one of the 'expatriate prostitutes.' This time I was wrong. Dallal is a fine young woman. And because she is a fine young woman in our silly society—"

Yusuf remembered that Zuhayr was hardly able to talk without using words like base, cruel, despicable, vile, cheap,

51

rude, son-of-a- —   and brother-of-a- —.

Zuhayr continued. "Our silly society. She is a fine young woman. And every fine young woman in these miserable circumstances is taking a gamble—risking her life and her future. I'll tell you that I predict a bad end for her. I see her ending up like Layla if she does not find someone who understands her. Or if someone who understands her does not find her. I care about you and I respect you and there is no need to repeat this a hundred times. I want you to understand this woman and not to push her to a bad fate like I did with Layla."

"Me! What do I have to do with her?" Yusuf answered in protest.

Irritation showed on Zuhayr's face. "Don't get angry and don't deny it. I told you before that you can lie to yourself, but not to me. I hear that this woman wanted you at her birthday party. She invited you last Thursday on this basis. She wanted you as protection from Morton White and from herself. She wanted you to save her from him, from her depending on him. Now I am sure that she is involved with her professor, but she wanted you to save her. And you—if you will allow me—you acted like any petit bourgeois would, someone whose true morals are no morals. It's cowardly. You saw her standing on the edge, and you pushed her to it when you should have pulled her from it, you should have—"

"Here we are back at your indictment of the petite bourgeoisie. Haven't we had enough of that?"

"Listen, I'm not accusing you of anything. I told you once that if I had only one virtue it would be that I do not pretend to be progressive but rather practice another morality. I practice my morals directly without covering up. I am able to admit my mistakes and make a scandal of myself. Listen, I am the one who pushed Layla to wander off and marry a spy. Oh yes, I am sure that Jean-Claude is a spy and I pushed her into his lap by being cowardly and stupid. Listen and understand me. Dallal is a respectable and suitable young woman. Work to understand her, try to comprehend her— she loves you and respects you. You can save her."

"I am neither the Messiah nor a charitable organization," Yusuf objected to Zuhayr, angry and annoyed that he was being so didactic. Zuhayr understood that Yusuf was trying to convince himself first.

"Listen, you have started refusing to listen. You only listen to your own voice," Zuhayr said. "You like to walk in the orchards and mountains of Yabrud and talk to yourself. You have started to forget that other people exist. You have forgotten how to debate. You have begun to forget the first lesson that we were taught in philosophy—debate and its goals, how to build your ideas, how to discover the truth by talking with other people. You think it is enough to talk only with yourself and to yourself. It's a disgusting habit. Talking only to yourself is like masturbation, it's intellectual masturbation. Listen to me, you've started to—"

Zuhayr's voice rose, making his true feelings and empathy with Yusuf's position clear. He had made some observations and objections about much of Yusuf's behavior, especially his solitude over the course of the past three years. This was the moment to be honest with Yusuf in order to help him escape from his isolation.

"This is not culture," he said. "You seek out contemplation, books, and movies—this is neither culture nor politics. This is, and I repeat, this is intellectual masturbation. You have started to reject people. All right, my friend. But who are you in the end? They will reject you like a worm. You must understand Dallal, and on the way to understanding Dallal, you will understand yourself and rebuild yourself. You will renew your connections with people. You need more friends than just me. Have you forgotten the energy you had when we met for the first time? Have you forgotten that what I liked about you was your generous heart and your ability to communicate? Have you forgotten that you always used to say that we should understand people, not judge them? Have you forgotten that knowledge is always a question, and that the question is always directed to others? Wake up, Yusuf! You are sinking into the abyss of hell, while thinking that you are simply watching others fall in, and you are taking malicious pleasure in it."

"I am sinking?"

"Yes sir, you are sinking. You think yourself a god who observes people and does not dirty his hands with the trivialities of the life of this world, only reading and wandering in the fields. I want to ask you why you left the party, and why you refused to give Dallal your protection. Why?"

Yusuf tried to lessen the building tension by joking, "I know... I'm sorry about Fawziya."

"Please, don't joke now. You know that Fawziya is not the problem. You are the problem. What is your problem? You made me scream in the streets like we were fighting. Let's go get a cup of coffee somewhere. Damn you, why do I have to deal with you anyway? Am I your mother? Your wife? Your grandmother? Your father? But forget the joking, before we change the subject I want to tell you that you are acting just like an Arab man. Like someone who is backward. Like a true coward."

"Dallal would be pleased to hear you accuse me of being a backward Middle Eastern man."

"She's right—she and Layla and Lamis and Fawziya and all the young women. What do we offer them other than a mirror image of our fathers' backwardness? We act as though we are only thieves or guards of their hymens. Let's leave them alone, brother. Let's leave them alone. Listen—"

"You seem pleased to play the role of professor today," Yusuf said. "Why don't you get a job teaching? It would be better—"

"Listen, we are a new generation," Zuhayr said. A generation that wants to be liberated. The generation of Dallal and Layla, Lamis and Fawziya. A generation that wants to grow by building on its experiences. To build another one like it. To brush off the ashes of this miserable Arab life. Men are not heroes anymore. Remember the heroes of great Arabic novels? Remember *A Bird from the East, The Saint's Lamp, Season of Migration to the North*, and *The Latin Quarter*? We have gone beyond the situations portrayed in them. What we have now is Jean-Claude and Morton White in our country. Our situation now is that Layla was attracted to Jean-Claude because I was one of the remnants of the past, or I acted as though I were. Dallal will go away with Morton White because you are even more of a coward than I was, and you are even worse because you refuse to learn from my experience."

"You bastard, you insult me as though I were—"

"My brother, I'm talking to you seriously. Listen now, I'm never going to repeat this serious conversation with you ever again, I swear. But for God's sake listen to me now. Take my desire to ramble on into account and listen to me. Understand me and don't act like a jealous, young lover. Try to understand what Dallal's relationship with Morton White means."

Yusuf felt a pinch in his heart when Zuhayr used the expression, "Dallal's relationship with Morton White," but Zuhayr continued without turning to look at Yusuf. It was as though he were talking to himself. "Understand her, try to comprehend her. Understanding *The Saint's Lamp, A Bird from the East, Season of Migration to the North,* or *The Voices of Suleiman Fiyad* does not make you smart. What would be smart is to understand Dallal. That's what I learned from my relationship with Layla, and what happened to her. That's what you refuse to learn because you—because you—I don't know what to say. Go inside, come on, this is the Dar Café. Please go in. I'll treat you to a glass of wine. Let's wet our lips, you've dried mine out, you son-of-a-bitch! Come on!"

"Enter, and may God grant you safe entry into—hell," Yusuf joked back.

"No, go to Dallal's house, and enter her heart. Tomorrow is Friday and you must visit her at home. She's an intelligent woman and will realize that your visit to her is an apology for your despicable behavior this evening." Then he winked and said, "And a birthday gift wouldn't hurt. How much more do I have to teach you?"

Minerva

Yusuf was convinced of the truth of Zuhayr's words. The pride he had inherited from his rural upbringing, however, made him act differently from his convictions and his conscience. He was convinced that Dallal was a fine young woman and that he should visit her Friday morning, but something made him feel unable to see her. And this impelled him to return to Yabrud Friday morning instead of visiting Dallal. It was not feelings of shyness toward Dallal or dislike of her that led him to run away from himself and from her, but now he could not define his feelings for her. And the situation was now marred by pettiness and wounded pride—he had to try to reclaim his self-respect!

Yusuf had planned his life in a way that was so different to how it was unfolding now that he could not experience these changes as a fresh breeze over the stagnant swamp that was his life. Perhaps deep down he was denying that Dallal was like a small stone that made a ripple in the lake that was himself. Yusuf had always arranged his affairs on the assumption that he would live alone. He would return to Tartus to fill an empty position teaching philosophy and live the life that he loved—going to his village, to Arwad, to coastal mountain villages. He would read, sit in seaside cafés, and attend party meetings knowing that he would not get anything out of them. He would be living with the people among whom he was born and raised.

Essentially, he dreamed of retreating into his cocoon. He did not realize that time would rip it open and throw him outside of it. Dallal had become a colorful butterfly dancing in front of him, after he thought his heart had died and his eyes had become blind to color. But now, here was his heart beating despite his careful planning, his decisions, and his projects, after he had thought that his heart would stop beating in the days when he was infatuated with Minerva.

In those days he was 22 years old and teaching in an elementary school. He was coming of age, learning about life, love, and politics in the countryside of Jazeera. This was the time of the 1967 June War and the early 1970s. Yusuf was one of the generation that felt truly defeated, but not at all responsible for the defeat. He would fight and be victorious. Along with his comrades, he would say that the country was defeated because the leaders were asleep, and because the people were excluded from the struggle for Palestine. There was an instant and magical prescription—all politics must do is be for the people. The prescription was simple and naïve to the degree that Minerva, a beautiful, young Assyrian woman, was convinced of it from the first moment Yusuf said this to her the first time they met. There was no need to have another political discussion with Minerva to persuade her of this, but rather a time came when he had to change the conversation and convince her of his love. Yusuf spent an entire year with Minerva—kind Minerva, Minerva as fresh as morning dew, shining Minerva, open like a rose. Minerva, Minerva.

Minerva had gotten married the following year to an engineer and had flown away with him to live in Canada. She left Yusuf trying to convince the party of his ideas, continuing his studies in philosophy at the university, and explaining his theories and ideas to every young man and woman whom he met. When Minerva left, she left behind a deep wound in his soul. Yusuf tried to not feel it. He tried to hide it both from the eyes of people around him and from

himself as well. Minerva left, leaving behind an emptiness in
Yusuf that he tried to fill by keeping busy with political
activities, party meetings, and reading.

It was during this time that Zuhayr, whom he met taking
university exams, described him as a machine. A machine
that believes that it thinks well because it babbles on a lot,
though it carries the capability for dangerous destruction
inside itself. This machine that was Yusuf carried a deep
sorrow and would explode after drinking a bottle of wine, or
after a heated conversation with Zuhayr or another friend.
Yusuf was afraid to indulge in this sorrow because at the time
he did not know what it would lead to. He was sad about
Minerva, about the days that passed, about a time that would
never come. Yusuf was sad about his world, his country, his
party—they had all begun to seem like an extinguished
candle that would never be lit again. At times he wished that
he could light it, even if he had to use the fire in his own eyes.

Yusuf felt a transparent sorrow about the present slipping
through his fingers like water, like sand or air. Little by little,
he started to surrender to his despair, accepting his destiny,
drowning in his isolation and deep sadness. Little by little,
Yusuf surrendered to his fate. He was a philosophy teacher
who did not hide his ideological and political leanings. He
read, visited a few friends, did not speak much, avoided
people, enjoyed strolling through the orchards of Yabrud
during the school year, and in his mountain village and along
the seashore in Tartus in the summer. He was just waiting for
the day he could return to teach in Tartus—return to the
seaside and the olive trees to finish what is left of his life. But
now he felt as though he were lost and what was coming
would not change anything.

Minerva used to call him the "reckless one." Where are

you Minerva—to see this emotional recklessness? Now, at 32, he has turned into a wise old man waiting for a ship to return, when it was he before any others who believed that it had sunk centuries and centuries ago. Where, oh where are you, Minerva, to see Yusuf?

Once he could not bear to be alone for even one minute, and now he is bored by any get-together with more than two people. He withdraws to wander through the orchards of Yabrud, the fields of his mountain village, or in the streets of Damascus. Where are you, Minerva, to see this Yusuf, who was once reckless like the winter sea, and now has become calm like the sea in autumn? Where are you, Minerva, to give your opinion about Dallal?

Yusuf had first met Dallal's parents in Damascus and remembered his distant relationship to them when he was in this state of limbo, when he had visited them and met Dallal. He was an extinct volcano who hoped to forget his days of constant eruption. Zuhayr, who had lived with him through the days of enthusiasm and discussions, had now come to remind him of those days. He had spent so much energy avoiding all obligations and organizations, and now Zuhayr was reminding him about his past. And his past recalled his present misery—the misery of his life and its uselessness. It was as though Zuhayr were reminding him that the one who does not progress will regress. He reminded Yusuf of his emptiness and disappointment; Zuhayr was a wake-up call, as though his consciousness, his hidden voice, the remains of the fire under the ashes, and Dallal were all absent. Was she just like Zuhayr? Trying unknowingly to rekindle the fire of his heart that Yusuf had tried to forget existed?

Yusuf opened the book that he had bought the other day, *The Age of Enlightenment*, and tried to read, to escape from both his memories and himself. He felt that his past and his present were alive and portrayed on every page of the book. He saw pictures on the pages but realized that he could not understand even one word. He closed the book, got up and made himself a cup of coffee, sat back down, and drank it, surrendering to the memories he had become addicted to. He knew exactly how they followed each other. He did not know how long he had been in this state of reverie and nothing would have brought him out of the flow of his memories were it not for the ringing doorbell. He opened the door and was surprised to see a police officer. He was frightened at first, but then remembered that they came as civilians if the political situation were tense.

"Are you Ustaz Yusuf?"

"Yes. Can I help you? What can I do for you?"

"Could you sign here please?"

Yusuf looked at the paper. It was a military call-up order.

Yusuf

Yusuf did not feel worried about being called up. Though the school year was coming to an end, at least he would not have to deal with exams, grading, and proctoring. He could return to the seashore and its cafés, knowing that he would do nothing in the army but read. This would put an end to this problem, which Yusuf did not quite know how he had found himself in the middle of—the problem that disturbed the tranquility of his quiet life and started to threaten his future plans. That is, if it were correct to call his decision to live a solitary life "future plans."

He thought about phoning Zuhayr to say that he had received a draft notice and then going directly to Tartus. But it would be better to go to Damascus first to see Zuhayr and take some gifts with him. He thought about visiting the chief sergeant's family, but said to himself, "I'm not going." He then relented and thought, "It's better to go, maybe they need something from Tartus or from the village." Then, "I'm not going to drop by. This is my chance to finish with the whole affair." Yusuf had begun to realize that Dallal's family wanted a serious relationship to develop between him and Dallal. Finally, he made up his mind to go to Damascus and visit Zuhayr, but not the chief sergeant's family.

Yusuf was in Damascus Sunday at noon. He called Zuhayr at the newspaper, they met and had lunch together, and agreed that Yusuf would come to Damascus on every break. Zuhayr said that Layla and Jean-Claude had asked about him last Friday at lunch in Dumar. He relayed to Yusuf that he had told Layla how recently Yusuf had been running away from himself, from him, and from a childish love affair.

"So you're still talking behind my back, you bastard!" Yusuf said.

Zuhayr countered, in a strange tone, that he had decided to tell only the truth from this day forward, God help him. He then asked quite seriously, "Aren't you going to say good-bye to Dallal?"

Yusuf was annoyed. "What does Dallal mean to me that I have to say good-bye to her?"

In order to change the subject, Yusuf told Zuhayr that he wished he could have seen Layla and Jean-Claude and had lunch with them on Friday, but that he had felt he needed to be alone. Yusuf asked him to say hi to Layla and Jean-Claude the next time he saw them. He then remembered Fawziya and added smugly, "And good sir, please also say hi to Mrs. Fawziya Sabbagh for me."

Zuhayr laughed and said that she had called in the morning just before Yusuf called and that they had agreed to have dinner together that evening.

Yusuf snorted a laugh. "Do you remember about your theory of the three kinds of prostitutes?"

"You're right," Zuhayr said, chuckling. "Fawziya's one of the second kind." He was quiet. Then, in a tone somewhere between seriousness and kidding, between lightheartedness and sorrow, he said, "But what I am unsure of is what type of prostitutes you and I are."

Yusuf said good-bye to Zuhayr and went to the Karnak bus station in Baramkeh. He would try to get a seat on the three o'clock bus. Failing that, he would go directly to the small bus station in Abassiyeen. When he did not find a seat on a Karnak bus as he had hoped, he hailed a taxi to take him to Abbasiyeen. Just as he opened the door, it struck him that he should go to the chief sergeant's house.

Maybe they needed him to do them a favor in Tartus or in the village. If the chief sergeant himself were home, he could ask him about the military situation, "To Mezzeh, my friend, please."

Chief Sergeant Yunis

Chief Sergeant Yunis was returning from the camp. He sat by himself in the front seat near the driver, thinking about Dallal. Lately, her entire temperament had changed—she had become sharp and short-tempered, went out at night and came home late, ignored her little brother, and constantly disagreed with Muhammad. She contradicted and tormented her mother and had even started contradicting her father, who had realized his educational aspirations and dreams through her. He loved and spoiled her and counted on her being raised in a conflict-free atmosphere. He had supported and promoted her independent personality amidst a family atmosphere of freedom, truth, confidence, and trust.

But now he had begun to doubt her honesty, and he felt that she had lied to him more than once, although he had pretended to believe her. He had even started to notice a certain disrespect in the way she talked to him. He did not know how she had turned out like this or how these changes had happened, but he felt them. He began to have doubts and suspicions for which he did not have tangible proof. He loved his daughter and wanted the best for her. He had done the best he could, everything he could, for her and her brothers, and now he felt that his daughter was slipping away from between his fingers. She was like a rose he had grown and cultivated and that now had started to wilt, although he had never failed to care for it, even for one night.

He wished that he could help resolve the situation between Yusuf and Dallal by hinting at the subject with Yusuf. But Yusuf had not come to visit last Thursday. Was Yusuf perhaps put off by his daughter's brusqueness? Maybe it would be best to ask Dallal directly about it, to act nicely with her.

He would invite her to go for a walk, sit with her in a park or some place, and talk to her about why she was changing. He would say to her, "Honey, we used to be friends. Sweetheart, I'm not like the other fathers. I am your friend, just as you always say. You are the oldest of your siblings at home while Muhsin is abroad. Why are you changing these days? What's going on with you? Are you overworked? Annoyed with your teaching? Quit the teaching hours. Leave yourself free to study. I don't want you to do anything except learn. I did my best in my life just for you children. I left the village, exiled myself to the military, and I do not like it. I spent twenty years on the front. Why did I do all of this? Why? If it weren't for you children, for your happiness, for your futures... Why have you started fighting with your mother? Why are you so short-tempered? Why do you hit little Ali? Why do you harass Muhammad? Even I myself have started to feel as though you do not respect me as you once did. Oh, my daughter! What do you want, Dallal? For God's sake!"

The car reached Mezzeh. The chief sergeant got out and walked toward his house. He reached the door and saw it ajar. He heard Yusuf's voice and was glad for a moment, but when he heard Yusuf's tone, he felt disheartened. "Ha ha, they are back to arguing," he said to himself.

"Please, don't try to take revenge on Arab men, on your assumptions about what Arab men are like, and, more specifically, on me," he heard Yusuf saying. "I know your type; you are the children of the petty bourgeoisie. You think that the revolution is cursing your family and your homeland and hurting your friends. You think that the revolution is a mutiny against the father and you forget—"

The chief sergeant walked into the hall that was used as a living room and stood listening as Yusuf went on. "The revolution should be in society, in consciousness, in—"

Dallal noticed that her father had entered the house. "Hi, Baba," she said.

Yusuf turned and the chief sergeant saw his angry face. The chief sergeant smiled and said, "Hello, Ustaz Yusuf, you find yourself in an argument again!" Then he turned to Dallal and asked, "Where is your mother? Where is Ali?"

The chief sergeant tried to add calm to the atmosphere after he seeing how these two faces glowered with anger. This must be a serious disagreement between his daughter and Yusuf. He saw something like rancor flashing in their eyes and this gave him pause.

"I forgot to make you coffee. Discussions make me forget," said Dallal. "What do you think, Baba? Will you have coffee with us or do you prefer to eat? I'm going out in five minutes. Should I make you something to eat quickly? Mama went to the neighbor's house to get Ali."

Dallal was speaking quickly, like someone who wanted to finish with something before a hurried departure. Chief Sergeant Yunis was upset by this. Perhaps Yusuf took her leaving as an outward lack of respect for him or perhaps Dallal intended this to insult him.

When his wife came in, he noticed that she did not welcome Yusuf as she usually did. Then he understood that she had been there at first and had left after Yusuf had arrived in order to give Yusuf and Dallal the opportunity to talk.

"How's the military situation these days?" Yusuf asked.

"Pretty bad. The situation is tense. I think war will break out again. We've had enough of these useless wars," the chief sergeant said.

"You are right. But they force it on us."

"True."

Yusuf was convinced that the Israelis would not attack. "I think it's just maneuvers to exercise political pressure, and, at the most, the government would be satisfied by a small operation in South Lebanon."

"And us, what will we do if this is the situation?" asked Chief Sergeant Yunis.

"We won't do anything—there is a tacit agreement which the Israelis and the Syrians will not violate."

"When wars break out, all of these agreements are for naught, Yusuf."

It sounded to Yusuf that Chief Sergeant Yunis had said his name, "Yusuf," with a caring tone. This was the first time that the chief sergeant had not called him "Ustaz Yusuf."

In the confident tone of someone deeply involved in international politics, Yusuf said, "No, for Syria the matter is complicated with international dimensions. The Soviet Union—"

The chief sergeant interrupted. "I do not think that Israel cares about anyone and I do not think that anyone is on our side. You progressives always talk about the Russians. The Russians have their own interests!"

Yusuf did not wish to have this political discussion; he already knew the chief sergeant's opinion on the subject. He looked at his watch—it was five o'clock. He noticed that Dallal was no longer there and had left without saying good-bye. He told the chief sergeant that he had been called up and that he was going to Tartus to join his unit. Did they need anything from the village?

The chief sergeant asked him just to send his regards to his family, and to find out from his brother Muhammad how far along the house being built in the village had come.

At the door, Yusuf said that he thought that a war would not happen. Umm Muhsin kissed Yusuf good-bye as though she were kissing her own son. She was unable to hide her warm feelings for him this time; it was the first time that she had kissed him. Yusuf kissed little Ali good-bye, also for the first time. As Yusuf shook Chief Sergeant's Yunis' hand, the chief sergeant said to him, "I hope that your opinion is more correct than mine this time. *Inshallah* war will not break out."

Morton White

Dr. Morton White was a drama professor who had graduated from Harvard University. His specialty was British drama in the 1950s, especially the Angry Young Men playwrights. His doctoral dissertation was on the plays of John Osborne.

He had reached the age of 35. He had married at 25, and by 30 was divorced from his wife Sally, a lecturer in the economics department. He lived alone in the house the university had given him. Every year in the summer, he traveled to a different country. In addition, he went to countries where he was invited to give lectures during the academic year. Last year, he had been invited to give a series of lectures on the Angry Young Men in the Department of English Literature at Damascus University. He liked Damascus and the admiration of the faculty and the students. They saw in him a quick-witted professor, experienced in teaching, and with wide knowledge. The university made an agreement for him to teach there during the 1981–1982 academic year.

Dr. Morton White liked to interact with other people. He was of average height, had a blond beard, and because of his openness was more similar in character to inhabitants of Mediterranean countries than inhabitants of the island of rain and fog. That year, he still carried a deep sadness within him and the feeling that Sally had left him because she was in love with another man. After he split up with Sally, Morton White had had numerous relationships, but deep down he still loved her. He tried to call her many times, and they had dinner together more than once, but she refused to love him. They saw each other less and less frequently until, finally, they stopped seeing each other all together.

Then he came to Damascus. After some time, he came to rebuild himself and to have time to do some research. He thought he could live a new and different life. He would get to know a new country and what better way to get to know a city or a country than through a woman?

Dr. Morton White was not comfortable with his Arab colleagues, although a few had graduated from the same university that he had. He felt that their information, knowledge, and curricula were behind the times. He noticed the troubled relationships between professors and students and continued acting as he pleased. If they did not like it, God had created many countries, and he had his own country.

He opened his home to his male and female students and their friends, like Ahmad Abd al-Sitar, Marwan Muhayri, Dallal, Fawziya, and Lamis, whom he was interested in when he first arrived in Damascus. She seemed overly self-conscious and serious to him, though. He then noticed that Dallal, even though she was serious, liked him. He could tell from the way she moved and her understanding way of listening to him talk, and because she visited considerably more frequently than the other female students. He felt her dislike of her Arab professors. At first he did not find her attractive, but with time he began to see her Middle Eastern beauty. When he was able to see her height, her long, soft, black hair, and her deep eyes, he started to feel a certain love for her. Dallal was sometimes worried and at other times calm. He thought of her as a typical Arab girl—she is shy and she wants things, but is not open about it. This is what made him cling to her more tightly; he had illusions that he would discover Arab women through Dallal. He would explore this

Middle East that was shrouded in secrets.

He felt that she had brought Yusuf to her birthday party as camouflage, or to make him understand that she had a special male friend. He was often astute in his understanding of people. He could see that she wanted to arouse his jealousy using Yusuf and arouse Yusuf's jealousy through him. He realized that she had a special affection for Yusuf. He could tell this from her depression after Yusuf left the party; he was sure of it when he witnessed her hysterical laughter as she tried to cover up her despondency. He thought, "She should enjoy me while I'm here and marry Yusuf after I'm gone."

He reproached himself, however, for having this idea. He had started to convince himself that he liked her and started to see her as a perfect companion, polite and kind, with whom he could stay up late and go on trips. She was a nice girl who did not argue with him or object to anything. She would go with him wherever he wanted, come to his house, ease his loneliness, go on picnics with him during the holidays, travel to other Syrian cities that she would like to visit. They would go to Aleppo. Over the course of time it would be fine with him if their relationship were to develop into love. By spending time with her, he would decide what the extent of their relationship would be. Would they continue to be together or would they stay within the limits of a teacher-student relationship? But then he thought, "I'm going to let her decide what her relationship with the other guy is. She is using her relationship with me to hide her relationship with Yusuf."

On Friday evening, the day after the party, he felt a desire to see Dallal. He wished that he knew where her house was so he could go to it. He remembered that once she declined to point out where her house was. He told himself, "These Arabs are masters of secrecy in everything, even the location of their houses!" He realized that he did not know anything about her except that she was a good student and that she had a strong personality compared to the others. He noticed that she did not say much about her private life and tried to seem like someone without secrets or special relationships. He also noticed that she wanted her relationship with him to stay within the boundaries of a teacher-student relationship—at least in front of the others. He told himself that she would definitely come to him. He was thinking about her while he was lying in bed, reading a new novel. He had started to doubt this, however, reflecting, "She might not come after I proposed that she spend the night at my house and she refused." He turned out the light to go to sleep while muttering to himself, "These Arabs are mysterious, it is difficult for a man to understand them."

As he settled his head on the pillow, he remembered Rudyard Kipling's famous quote that left him totally unconvinced, "East is East and West is West, and never the twain shall meet." He remembered his desire to see Dallal outside of class, so he amended Kipling's words, "No, they can meet. It is possible. But when will that happy time be?"

Dallal

Dallal left her house without saying good-bye to Yusuf and not knowing where she would go. She thought about going to the movies but did not really feel like it. She thought about going over to Fawziya's place, but she knew that Fawziya was with Zuhayr now and that they were eating dinner together. Dallal did not approve of Fawziya's quick way of responding to invitations and forming relationships, but she was envious of her private life, her experience, and her nonchalance about sex.

She had a secret desire to live like Fawziya, but the way she was brought up did not allow her to let her sexual repression explode, as had happened with Fawziya. She remained divided—between her eternal desire for absolute freedom, which was her friend's style, and her desire for the true love that every girl dreams about, just like any girl who has emotions and a progressive mentality and who cannot find a man to envelop in her love. She had never found a man she thought worthy of the generous love she had to offer or even deserving of her emotions. Dallal confided to the people closest to her that she felt superior to all her girlfriends, except Lamis al-Muradi.

She felt the instability and weakness of character of the people who surrounded her—especially the young men who taught and studied alongside her. These young men could sense her superior attitude and felt she was pretentious. In the end, she was convinced that she was superior to everyone, more mature than others her age and that no man deserved her or her love. Her criticisms of men were exaggerated—men are silly, men are nasty—and she tried to hide her true longing for a man who would love and understand her.

She had started to become a true student of Faiza, Fawziya's mother, without realizing it, until one day when Yusuf had appeared on her doorstep. Yusuf seemed to be a complex personality—otherwise why had he remained unmarried until now? She had heard about him, knew about him, and was sure that he had experienced many relationships in his life. He had alluded to a few transient relationships in his conversations with her. She thought he would try to play her for the fool just as he had tried to do with the others. Yusuf, however, did not give her any signals, playful or polite, and so, to herself, Dallal thought him to be icy cold. Eventually, she began to think that he was conceited and a loathsome, snobby person who should be humiliated. But she still wanted to see and talk to him. After a while, she was able to relax and announce to Lamis al-Muradi that Yusuf was a young man with a complex—like all Arab men. She had seen the proof of this herself when he left Morton White's party.

When she left her house, she did not realize that she was going directly, consciously or not, to the professor's house. She did not know how she found herself ringing the doorbell. After he opened the door and she fell into his arms, the professor said to Dallal coolly, "I knew you would come today, tomorrow, or the day after. That is how you Arab women are."

He looked at her with a mixture of pity and passion. "I know why you didn't stay here with me on your birthday night. You were embarrassed in front of Fawziya."

Dallal felt insulted. She shuddered. "No, I do what I want and what I believe in; I am not afraid. No one makes me feel embarrassed."

Morton White came closer to her and stroked her hair, his hand moving down to her neck. He put his arms around her and started to kiss her. Dallal thought, "I'm going to stop and see what he wants." She was not used to this type of flirtation. "Please, I beg you," she said. "Get away from me, I did not come here for this. Let's have coffee. I was walking down your street, so I decided to come by your place."

Morton White felt that she was lying and making up excuses. He realized that she had stumbled. He knew her personality and that the reason she was so happy was her independence and her desire to seem like a liberated, un-Arab, hard-to-get, young woman in front of him. But he could see that she was running away from her true self.

"No, you were embarrassed by Fawziya. Let's drink something other than coffee."

He prepared tea and brought two glasses. After pouring the tea, he leaned over and again put his arms around her. "You are a very sweet girl, but the problem with Arab women is that they are full of complexes. They are afraid of others and forget that they themselves also have the right to live."

He was not deceiving her. He did think that she was nice, but this is what he thought about all Middle Eastern women.

Dallal listened to him and told herself that he was right. She was silent and let him do what he wanted. She let everything go without caring. She did not know how she found herself in his bed—both of them naked. She felt neither pleasure nor pain. She was perplexed because she found herself thinking of Yusuf. The whole situation felt like a dream. The only things that convinced her that what had just happened was reality were the few drops of blood splattered on the bed and Morton saying that the shower was ready.

They got out of bed. She asked for a cup of coffee.

Perhaps because she still felt as though she were dreaming, in a trance, she said to Morton White while the two of them were drinking coffee, "Hey, Morton White, you never told me what you thought of Yusuf. The philosophy teacher I introduced you to." She thought her tone was innocent, but he understood what was behind her question.

"Nice guy, though he seems spiteful and a bit impatient. He has the face of an American cowboy, and his clothes—" Morton White smiled.

Dallal listened intently.

"No, there is no way that guy is a philosophy teacher!" Morton White stopped for a moment and then added, "Unless philosophy teachers in your country are like that!"

Chief Sergeant Yunis

When Dallal got home she still felt as if she were in a trance.

"Why are you so late this time?" Chief Sergeant Yunis asked. "It's one o'clock in the morning!"

"I'm exhausted, leave me alone," Dallal said. "I want to go to sleep."

Her father was enraged by this answer and tried to get hold of himself. "I am not asking you how you feel," he said. "I want to know why you are so late!"

"I do not want anyone to speak to me," Dallal said. "I'm so tired."

Chief Sergeant Yunis felt insulted. All the love he had for her in his soul, as well as all of his years of service in the army, were aroused inside of him. The love of family on which he was raised and that he had tried to cultivate in Dallal was also stirred. "If you do not want anyone to talk to you, you should live alone. In this house we will talk with you and you will talk with us," he said angrily.

He struggled to restrain his temper. His body began to tremble and he started to feel as though he had no limbs. He heard Dallal saying that she would live alone then and that she could not stand anyone. He heard her mother ask her worriedly, "Dallal! What are you saying?" He tried to keep himself calm, but in order to keep her away from him until his anger had subsided, he said, "Get out of here!"

He heard her answering him with hysterical screams, "I will not get out of here! I will be a thorn in your eyes. I hate you!" He heard her repeat, "I hate you! I hate this marriage that you have cooked up for me, I hate this Yusuf! I want to live my life alone, I want to learn, I want to travel, I want to leave this awful country!"

As Dallal raised her voice, her father's anger began to increase. His hand began to feel light and he lost control. He did not even know what he had done, but he heard his daughter saying, "You hit me—you hit me! Even *you* hit me. You are just as disgusting as all the others. All you men are nasty and despicable. You hit me!"

This was the first time she had ever been slapped. It jolted her from her screaming and hysteria to a volcanic explosion of tears and anger. She rushed to the door, shrieking. "I am not going to live with you, I will not live in this stinking, revolting country!"

Dallal opened the door and rushed outside. Her mother followed her, wailing. "Dallal, be reasonable—come back!"

"Let her go," Chief Sergeant Yunis yelled at his wife. "Leave the little whore alone. Just let her go."

"Yunis, Yunis! What is the matter with you?" Dallal's mother felt bewildered. "You've gone mad, Yunis. Dallal, come back—be reasonable!"

Meanwhile Yunis kept roaring over and over, "Go to hell! Go to hell! Go to hell!"

Then the terrible silence of the night began. When Yunis looked around, certain that Dallal had left, he felt empty inside. Tears came to his eyes, and then he heard his disconnected sobbing become a howling cry.

Yusuf

Two days after Yusuf joined his army unit, the attacks began. The Israelis first attacked South Lebanon, then the Syrian missile bases in the Beqa'a, and then the Syrian forces in Jezin. They rushed in with their tanks threatening to occupy the Beqa'a and then hit Syria in the middle, dividing it into two parts at Homs. Yusuf was camped out in the first artillery unit near the oil port between Baniyas and Tartus on the Syrian coast. They had been warned several times and were on alert, but the enemy never showed up on the coast.

Yusuf started following the news on the radio, wondering what Zuhayr was thinking, what he and others thought about the war. A full-scale war could break out at any moment, and he surprised himself by thinking about Dallal. What was she thinking? What had happened between him and Dallal? Was it anything serious that he should be thinking about her now? Who is this Dallal to him that he should wonder and care about what she thought about this very grave and dangerous situation?

One day, a new officer approached Yusuf, asking if he thought the war would develop further or if it would be confined to limited clashes.

"No, I don't think the war will worsen, despite the continuing clashes," Yusuf answered.

"Why don't we open fire on the Golan front?" the officer asked him.

Yusuf felt this question was ridiculous. "Do you think a full-scale war is easy? We are not ready. In reality, we do not want it, and we may not be capable of it."

"You are wrong," the officer said. "It's just that the Russians will not let us. They don't give us good weapons or enough of them. Look, can't you see how the bombs fall down like paper?"

Yusuf laughed. "I fear that we, not the missiles, are paper," he said.

"But many people in the country are excited about the Russians because they do not know anything," the officer said.

How pointless it was to have this recurring conversation, when all Yusuf wanted was to be alone with his thoughts. He grew silent and did not answer the young officer so as to make him understand that he wanted to be alone.

The officer left him and returned to his platoon, and Yusuf's concerns about the missiles came back. He remembered Ahmad Abbud saying, "It's more serious because it's not clay pots but missiles this time." He told himself that he would pass by Ahmad Abbud's shop today or tomorrow to see who was working in his place—to see if it were really closed up or if someone else had opened it.

Yusuf remembered Damascus and Yabrud; he thought about Zuhayr; he thought about Dallal. He remembered her telling him that Morton White said that war would break out. He remembered that he himself had been convinced that war might break out and that this was the opposite of Zuhayr's opinion. He thought about the party at Morton White's house and he started to feel badly about having left the party early. "Why should I have stayed? What is my relationship to those people?" he questioned himself. "Why should I have stayed and spent the evening with the others?" He recalled Lamis al-Muradi's face and her even temperament, and once again he felt that he should not be thinking about Dallal. Why did the two of them bother each other so much? Why did he explode at her again? He thought that he had begun to understand her. "She was upset with me because she thought I was going behind her back and conspiring with her parents to marry her." He gave himself a little lecture: "But she is wrong. Fawziya has definitely influenced her."

He felt that he now understood why she had left the house without saying good-bye to him. "She wanted to make me understand that I was her parents' guest and not her guest." He reproached himself once more for being cruel when he talked to her, and then again for feeling bad for being tough. He thought, "Who is she? Just a pretentious little girl." He corrected himself though. "No, that's not true. To be fair, she is a fine young woman. She is kind and intelligent, but she is inexperienced in life."

He remembered when he was her age and thought that it was always better to quarrel with a person who was older than you. He felt like seeing her. He promised himself that he would visit her when he went to Damascus. She would understand his visit as an apology. He wondered, "What is happening with her father these days? Did he really retire like he wanted to and return to the village to live in the house that was almost ready?"

His thoughts returned to the battle in Beirut and Zuhayr's opinion that the war would be a conclusive battle. Israel would demolish the existence of the Palestinians in Lebanon. Then he remembered Zuhayr's nasty comment about Yusuf's own opinion, "Basically, the resistance killed itself in Beirut and doesn't need Israel to do it for them anymore." He remembered his visit to Beirut last year with Zuhayr and their common conclusion about the situation of the Palestinians. Dallal interrupted these thoughts once again, though, "I wonder what she is doing now? Is she still seeing Morton White now that the academic year has ended? Did he deepen his relationship with her?" He felt twinges of pain in his chest when the idea of Dallal and Morton White's relationship came to his mind. He whispered to himself, "Damn them, what do I have to do with them?" He felt a kind of sorrow stealing into his heart and he thought of Minerva.

A soldier called out for everyone to get ready; the army shuttle bus that took the soldiers home had arrived. Still lost in though, he got on the bus, thinking all the way to Tartus. He passed by Mashbaka and bought a sandwich. He ate it and went to the bus station to wait for the bus to his village. He remembered that he had decided to pass by Ahmad Abbud's shop to see if it was really closed up. He walked toward Salhiyyeh Street. From the end of the street, he could see that the shop was open, so he went in. Ahmad Abbud was standing right there. "Hello, Comrade," he said to Ahmad.

This word was a joke between Ahmad and Yusuf. Ahmad used the word in order to tease him for still having the same ideas that he had in high school. Yusuf used the very same word to show it had the same meaning now as it did then.

"Hello and welcome, Comrade Yusuf! Come in, please come in," Ahmad said.

"What happened to your call-up?" Yusuf asked.

An old, caring love and friendship was still there. The bond that existed between Ahmad and Yusuf was the type that exists between people who have known each other since childhood and throughout their young adulthood. Ahmad had a true love and respect for Yusuf, the kind of respect you have for someone whose honesty you believe in totally. He was the kind of person whom you admire for having a fixed and solid opinion even if you disagree with it.

"I paid to get out of it."

Yusuf was surprised by the answer. "What? How?"

Ahmad laughed. "The easy way. We paid, Comrade. We paid ten thousand Syrian pounds. That's what I make in one month. Imagine if they took me to Lebanon and I stayed there all summer! I would have lost more than one hundred thousand pounds."

Yusuf could not find anything to say to Ahmad except to mutter, "True, I see. You're right. Just like that... Good-bye."

Then he turned and walked to the bus stop for the village.

Yusuf

The summer full of battles, killings, and political declarations passed. Yusuf reflected, "This is the fate of my generation. I am from this country and I live in this era. It is how I must live—through wars and lies, among murderers and secret agents. I will be prohibited from experiencing solace, love, and how to live a happy life."

Minerva continued to occupy his memories more than usual. Though he was only thirty-two years old, Yusuf began to see himself as an old man whose life had been for nothing. He was just waiting to die. In between the time he spent reading and at coffee shops, he was drowning in memories and sorrow. The army had begun to seem boring, and he spent more and more time AWOL from his unit; the commander of his unit was a classmate from his university days and had always liked Yusuf, so he overlooked his absences.

Yusuf thought more than once about going to Damascus, but he did not go despite his sincere desire to see Zuhayr. In the depths of his soul, Yusuf was afraid that he would not be able to stop himself from visiting the chief sergeant's house, as had happened the day he was called up. He started to feel nervous just at the idea of seeing Dallal once again. He covered up his fear, sometimes with hateful feelings and other times with superiority. He wished that Zuhayr would come visit and resume writing articles, carrying out investigations and having meetings with the soldiers where they were stationed in Lebanon. He tried to understand what his friend's opinion truly was by reading between the lines of the traditional, repetitive rhetoric of newspaper writing. Had his opinion changed? Did he feel he had won because he had predicted the situation correctly and war had broken out? Zuhayr had been thinking about a war of missiles and Soviets; what would he say about all this? He asked himself more than once, "Did Zuhayr ever see Dallal again? How has his relationship with Fawziya progressed?"

He wished that Zuhayr could be with him in Tartus so they could sit together every evening by the seaside or in the village, instead of being alone. He thought about how his long absence from Tartus made him feel that he no longer knew anyone. He thought about his school friends—how they had changed. Mazin Husayni had become a lieutenant colonel and the leader of his unit, Ahmad Abbud had become a businessman, Abd al-Fatah al-Amra worked in Damascus and Sa'id Qasim in Kuwait, Fu'ad Khalil was busy with his family.

The old boardwalk by the sea had been removed. The china trees that lined the street had been cut down. The Manshiyyeh Coffee Shop had closed down. What remained in Tartus? What was left of it? Now it was another Tartus to which he felt no connection. He felt like any Damascene or Yabrudi: he came, looked at the sea, and rode a boat to the island of Arwad. He remembered that he had once invited Dallal to visit Arwad and she had never responded.

Yusuf was walking on the new seaside boardwalk, busy thinking, as he did almost every evening that he did not go to the village, when he heard the horn of a car. He turned to look. There was Major Mazin Husayni calling out to him from the window of his car where he sat with his wife and kids. "Yusuf... Yusuf... Congratulations!"

"Congratulations? Why?" Yusuf was surprised.

"They released all the teachers! Come by tomorrow and turn in your gear."

The next morning Yusuf turned in all his gear and by

noon he was boarding the bus for Damascus. At five, he had arrived in Damascus and was knocking on Zuhayr's door.

The two friends did not shake hands, but rather pounced on each other and gave each other a long bear hug. They then retired to the living room. Glancing around, Yusuf spied some of his books in one of the corners and felt as though he were coming home. He then noticed the door of the bedroom opening and saw Fawziya walking toward him. The makeup on her face appeared newly applied. Zuhayr laughed and said, "I don't think you two need to be introduced."

"How are you doing Sitt Fawziya?" Yusuf asked her, thinking about Dallal. He heard Zuhayr's voice saying that he would prepare coffee. Yusuf felt uncomfortable at being left alone with Fawziya. He wanted to ask her about Dallal but was able to hold his tongue.

Fawziya knew what he was thinking, however, and waited for him to ask. When he did not, she knew that he did not want to admit it. Because of this she decided to broach the subject directly. "Why don't you ask about Dallal? Do you know what happened to her or doesn't that mean anything to you?"

Yusuf was surprised by the question. He had been thinking about the exact same thing. He said coldly, "It was perfectly normal that I knew her. Her parents are from my village."

"Well, she used to talk to me about you a lot," Fawziya said.

The words "used to" surprised Yusuf. He looked into Fawziya's eyes, wanting her to continue.

"Dallal is in Britain," Fawziya said.

Yusuf felt that his heart had dropped through his body and landed on the ground next to his feet.

Fawziya continued when she saw the color of Yusuf's face. "You are responsible for this."

"Me? What do I have to do with it?" Yusuf asked.

"You are responsible because you are a—" She paused for a moment before continuing. "A coward."

"What right do you have to talk to me like that?" Yusuf asked angrily.

"Excuse me, but it is not my opinion I am giving. This is how Dallal described you," Fawziya replied coldly.

Zuhayr came in, carrying the cups of coffee. They drank it, changing the topic of conversation. Fawziya excused herself, saying that she was late to meet her mother and if she were late her mother would throw her son out onto the street. She then turned to Yusuf, "I need to have a long talk with you. I'll see you here tomorrow at noon."

Playing the coquette, she said to Zuhayr, "Do you mind if we meet here tomorrow at your place?"

"Does that mean I should leave the house empty for you two?" Zuhayr laughed.

Fawziya was solemn. "No, it's better if you are here. You are always fooling around. You know very well what the discussion will be about and you even have an opinion about it."

After Fawziya left, Yusuf questioned Zuhayr, "Are you seeing Fawziya a lot?"

"I sleep with her a lot," Zuhayr responded in a crass tone.

Yusuf was laughing as he hugged him once again, "You bastard! Son-of-a—"

"Come on, let's go out tonight!" Zuhayr said. "I have a surprise for you that will show you that I have been thinking of your future even when you are away. Damn it. Am I your father, you son-of-a bitch? Let's go. Come on! I miss drinking with you."

Zuhayr

Yusuf longed to wander the streets of Damascus. He had drunk a lot the night before with Zuhayr. They had argued and debated, agreed and disagreed, gone home together exhausted, and fallen asleep quickly.

This morning he was again feeling that he needed to be alone in order to make a decision, so he went out to walk. Zuhayr's words to him last night were still in his mind. After their discussion had become quite heated, Zuhayr said straightforwardly, "Don't be a fool, come to Damascus. Stop dreaming about Tartus and your village. After today, look forward and don't look back. Your future is in Damascus, not Tartus. Moving to Damascus means guaranteed success. There is a job opportunity here. A school inspector who is a friend of mine promised me he would help. He agreed to do me the favor because you are my friend. Starting this school year, you will be in Damascus. I will give your answer to the inspector. You will live with me until you find a place. You'd be crazy not to agree."

The idea was new to Yusuf and he met it with the kind of resistance a person would at the first mention of a totally unexpected idea, especially an idea that contradicted all of his dreams, plans, and thoughts. It was true that Yusuf had gotten fed up in Tartus and the village this summer, but this did not affect his previous plan to come back and settle down in Tartus when circumstances allowed. He told himself that he was still coming and going only because he had not yet settled down, and perhaps also because he had to serve in the army, and because of the long period he had spent away. But he believed that he would feel settled and secure after he had returned forever. After he had drowned in the vortex of life and work.

He remembered Zuhayr saying to him angrily, "A reactionary is someone who dreams about the past. A progressive dreams about the future. What's the matter with you? Do you want me to keep reminding you of this truism? Tartus is your past and Damascus is your future. Understand me and understand me well. The transfer to the school in Damascus is ready. What is there for you in Tartus, my friend? You drove me crazy with your talk about Tartus and the village until we saw it last year. We went there, we saw it, and in two hours we were bored. It is a good place for a person to go, spend a couple of days, or even a week. But to live in that cemetery is a crime. Think about it! Or have you forgotten how to use your mind? Think, you—"

A female voice interrupted his thoughts. "Hello, Ustaz Yusuf."

Surprised, he looked up and saw a beautiful face that he had seen somewhere before. He could tell that the young woman knew that he did not remember her well. He felt uneasy.

"You definitely have forgotten. I am—"

The awful party at Morton White's house flashed through Yusuf's mind at that moment, and he interrupted her with a smile. "Oh… please do excuse me, you are Lamis. How are you Aniseh Lamis?" To sound a bit more formal, he added, "And how is your work these days?"

She smiled back. Yusuf seemed to want to keep talking to her so she stood with him and answered that she was teaching in a private school.

The pair was standing near Arnus square in the center of town. He did not know quite how he managed to suggest that they get a cup of coffee at the nearby Ya Marhaba Café. She did not know how or why she agreed. They went in and each ordered a cup of coffee. By the time they left the café, they had agreed to meet the next day—"Seven in the evening, here."

Fawziya

In the afternoon, Fawziya came carrying an apple. She had quit her part-time teaching at the middle school and had started working at an airline company. They had lunch together, she and Zuhayr and Yusuf. Through the conversation over lunch she discerned that Zuhayr had not yet talked to Yusuf about Dallal. Though she felt apprehensive about it, she brought up the subject while they were drinking coffee. "Do you know what happened to Dallal after you were called up by the army?"

"No, I haven't heard anything about her since that time," Yusuf answered, feeling a little tense.

"Then listen. One evening, she came to my house after one o'clock in the morning. She was crying and screaming like a crazy person, 'They hit me. They threw me out. I need a safe place to stay. I want to see Yusuf. By God, go with me tomorrow to Tartus! They kicked me out! Imagine that. Imagine, even my father beat me.' After I gave her some herbal tea to drink, she calmed down considerably. She spent the night at my place, and in the morning she asked if I minded if she stayed with me for a while, until she found a room to rent."

Fawziya went silent for a moment and then continued. "Of course my mother and I welcomed her. She did not come back that evening, and so I thought that maybe she had gotten a hold of herself and gone home. The next day, she came and slept at our place, on the third day she did not sleep at our place, and on the fourth day she said that she was going to tell me a secret. 'When I'm not at your place, I'm at Morton White's house. Tomorrow I'm going with him to Tadmor before he returns to Britain. He promised me that he would me invite me for a two-week stay at his place in London. I beg you, please do not tell anyone! Especially my family and Lamis al-Muradi. If they ask you about me, tell them you haven't seen me. I'm going to Britain; I think that Morton White has started to fall in love with me. I am hoping that things between us will develop further and that we will move in together. I'm going to get out of this miserable country.' I advised her to be more patient and think carefully about this—I suffered from the consequences of love and a rushed marriage, a marriage that happened as a reaction to something else. But she was involved with this professor."

Zuhayr broke in, "Her strong attachment to Morton White was her only defense against the predicament that she found herself in—"

"It is you all who dropped her, just like you drop every young woman," Fawziya added aggressively. "Tell him what happened to you, Zuhayr."

Zuhayr began, "Listen, my friend. One day a woman's voice that I knew I had heard before called me at the newspaper. She introduced herself, 'I'm Dallal, I don't know if you remember me.' She asked if she could visit me and arrived a half-hour later. Her face looked different than it had at Morton White's party. She said, 'I was thinking that I could get to know the newspaper business through you. Perhaps I could get a job here, I'm sick of teaching.' I could tell that she was thinking of you and came because she knew that you and I were friends. I acted as you always do in dealing with people and pretended that I had no idea why she was really visiting me. She then said, 'It seems that it's going to be a hot summer! Weren't you called up for military

93

service like your friend?' I noticed that she said 'your friend' scornfully trying to hide her true feelings. I was sure that she had come to ask about this friend but that her pride stopped her. She said good-bye and left without asking about you. Then she said that she would call or come by another time, but she did not and I never saw her again. You finish, Fawziya."

Fawziya picked up where he left off. "There's nothing more that needs to be said. Dallal came back and stayed with me most of the time. Her pride and dignity stopped her from staying at Morton White's house even though she went over there almost every day. She did not tell him about her fight with her parents although she was practically homeless. He invited her to stay with him in Britain for two weeks. She had enough money from her part-time teaching to pay for her ticket, and she sent me these postcards. She never sent any letters. Here, have a look."

On one postcard there was a picture of London Bridge, Big Ben, and one of the royal palaces. There was also a picture of Dallal standing in front of the door of a restaurant. Written on the front window was:

Welcome!
Ahlan wa Sahlan!
We Speak Arabic
Meat Here Slaughtered According to Islamic Shari'a Law

On the back of the picture Dallal had written, "I am the 'we' who speaks Arabic and slaughters the chickens according to Islamic Shari'a law."

Yusuf felt as though a knife had been plunged into his heart. He looked into Zuhayr's eyes and saw the sorrow that he knew was always there when he felt true pain. Through his sorrow, Yusuf heard Zuhayr announcing, as though it were his own inner voice, "She is paying the price for our mistakes."

Yusuf wanted to say something. "She is paying the price for the backwardness of our society, the price of the stage we have arrived at, the private—"

Zuhayr blew up in his face angrily. "Don't give me your philosophy about life! She is paying the price for *our* mistakes, us specifically. You and me and everyone like us. Us—us. We are the fourth kind of prostitutes."

"But why did she go away with the British guy?" Yusuf asked.

"She's free," Zuhayr answered, drowning in anger.

"One time I asked her if she would marry a foreigner, someone who was not Arab," Fawziya said. "And she answered, 'I don't want to separate my emotions and my life on the basis of patriotism.'"

"So where is the British guy?" Yusuf asked anxiously.

"He moved to the university in Cairo this year," Fawziya said and then turned to Zuhayr, "Did you give Yusuf his gift yet?"

Zuhayr went to the closet, muttering that this was yet another story. He opened it and took out a white shirt. "Listen my friend. Layla was here last week after she and Jean-Claude had spent a week in London. She told me that they were wandering around Soho. Down one of the streets, they saw a restaurant that had a sign on the door saying that they spoke Arabic and slaughtered meat according to Islamic traditions. They thought it would be a laugh to go in. While they were there talking to the waitress, they mentioned that they were going to Damascus and that Layla was Arab. When the waitress learned that Layla was Damascene, she was even more welcoming and refused to accept any money from them for the bill. Through them she sent a gift to my address—it was two shirts and a note saying, "One shirt is for Zuhayr and the other is for Yusuf." It doesn't take a genius to figure out the identity of the Arabic-speaking waitress in that restaurant in Soho.

Lamis al-Muradi

Lamis al-Muradi was a 30-year-old, Arabic-language teacher. She was single and did not talk much, and in this she was the opposite of the other teachers in the school. She had creamy white skin, was of average height, and wore prescription glasses over her beautiful eyes. She wore her clothes carelessly, which gave a certain elegance to her outward appearance. It was clear to anyone who stared into her eyes that behind her attractive looks and forthright manner of speaking, she guarded a hidden secret when talking to the outside world. She withheld something, even from herself; she pretended to have forgotten her secret so that she would in fact forget it.

Lamis was known for her exaggerated seriousness, for smoking a lot, and for hating alcohol—other than beer. She looked at trivial conversations about clothes and food with contempt, but was always happy when she saw two lovers together. Whenever she sensed trouble she would try to get involved, or invite the couple to her house for tea. She would always ask them, "When are you two going to get married? When will we celebrate your happiness?"

She would ask them this question hesitantly and insist with a sort of shyness. This was a shyness that she had known from the time she turned twenty years old, from the day she fell in love with Marwan. Marwan was her classmate. He was very academically talented and also politically involved. Then he abandoned everything—both her and his ideals— and went to continue his studies in France at the expense of the government, his ideas, and his political commitment. Once there, he simply reneged on his obligation to the government at whose expense he had studied. He renounced his ideals, married a Frenchwoman, and worked as a lecturer at Strasbourg University.

As for Lamis, her father died the year of her graduation, and the school refused to allow her to participate in the competition for positions for teachers because of her political beliefs, ideas she held because of Marwan. As a result, she was forced to leave Syria and work in Kuwait to support her two younger brothers.

Lamis lived in Kuwait for five years; it was there that she came to know the dryness of the desert. She lived with a dryness of the heart and even knew dryness of the soul. It was in Kuwait that she came to understand the taste of longing for home, longing for her mother, as well as the bitter taste of passionate longing for a betraying lover, for a lover who did not come.

In Kuwait, many people tried to exploit her or intrude into her lonely existence. But with time, she dug in deep to protect the essence of herself and to protect the ideas that were merged with the memory of her love—the love that had begun to reveal itself like an apparition passing through time, or an existence that was not this existence. Who knows, perhaps she was protecting a vague hope within herself for a love that would reawaken her heart and her soul.

With time, however, she lost all hope. She also lost her tenderness and her laugh. She who had lived for so long with a dryness of the heart and soul had lost the ability to understand any kind gestures or to care for anyone who would show kindness. Little by little, Lamis al-Muradi became convinced that she should play the role that she had sketched out for herself after her defeat—a haughty, lonely woman who had no place for trivial things, love or anything that resembled it in her life. She had sacrificed the beginning of her life—her youth—for her parents, and she would sacrifice the rest for the triumph of her ideas.

Some said about her, "She is a spinster who spends her time with politics instead of love, knitting, and gossip." Others accused her of having a wild and brazen secret love life. Still others had pity on her. She had a certain charm that made them all sympathize with her and her dedication. They forgot about her when she was not there; she regarded them all equally and she dealt with them seriously, respectfully, and with a hidden sorrow that said to everyone who understood human nature, "I seem like this, but I am not like this. It is just that I cannot change the picture that I drew of myself. Why don't you help me change it?"

Nobody dared to try seriously to help Lamis change her image of herself. Most people believed that she actually was the way that she presented herself to the outside world and didn't make an effort to get to know her. A few people, however, saw that there was more to her. George, for example, one of the nice people who worked with her, tried to flirt with her once, and she drove him away. He took her refusal to heart, apologized for his behavior, and married her classmate Su'ad. Her comrade in the party, Haysam, like most people who worked in politics, was not interested in— and perhaps knew nothing about—human emotions. Because of these things, Lamis al-Muradi's sorrow and loneliness began to increase. She started to become like the trunk of a tree, with dry, dead bark, like a rose whose petals have wilted. Who would be able to see the sap that flowed behind the dry bark?

Lamis knew the story of Dallal's and Yusuf's relationship. She wished that she could have played some role in helping it. She had tried to encourage Dallal to think more like she did. On more than one occasion, she had suggested that Dallal visit her with Yusuf so that she could meet Yusuf and explain Dallal's true feelings for him. The waters had run in another river, though; Dallal went to Britain and Yusuf had lost touch with her. But today she ran into Yusuf coincidentally. Why not have a chat with him? Why not talk with him about his romance?

Lamis al-Muradi

Seven o'clock at Ya Marhaba and Yusuf found that Lamis had arrived before him. He was amazed by her beauty; it was as though he were noticing it for the first time.

He greeted her and sat down across from her. He found it difficult to start talking to her, and as always happened in these situations, they talked about the usual things they both knew about. They then noticed that the sky was covered with clouds. Lamis said that it was going to rain and Yusuf replied, "I wish it would because I miss winter weather." Lamis said she could tell that he was in a low-spirited mood and that depressed people normally like winter. Yusuf was stunned that Lamis spoke to him as though she were someone who knew his temperament and moods. He wanted to ask her about Dallal but restrained himself. Finally he compromised. "Do you remember the party that we both attended?"

He thought he could use the party to get to the topic of Dallal in a roundabout way.

"I do remember it. Why did you and your friend run away so early?"

"We were busy."

"No you weren't. You were jealous of the English professor. Dallal was a good friend of mine and told me everything about you. I hear that she is in Britain, but I guess you know that." Yusuf pretended not to know. Lamis continued. "She sends me postcards from time to time. She used to talk about you with hidden admiration. At one time I thought that she was in love with you, and when I asked her she denied it. She used to say that there was this guy who was one of the best of all the guys she had met, but she didn't know why the two

101

of you always fought whenever you got together. She brought me to the movies to introduce me to you. To her friend with the strong personality, she said. That's why we were so surprised that you ran away."

"I didn't run away. I was busy. Besides, my relationship with her was that of a distant relative. What do I have to do with her crowd of friends?"

Yusuf was trying to avoid admitting to any relationship he had with Dallal.

"I know, I know… but you were the only one who could have saved her from her dilemma," Lamis said. "You were the only one she truly loved. She never told me this; her pride stopped her. Just as her pride is stopping her from returning home now that the professor has abandoned her. She would not come back even if she wanted to, not now at least. Dallal is the type who thinks that being stubborn and hiding your emotions makes for a strong personality. She is the type that cannot admit or face up to a mistake. I understand her—and you must understand her. But you fled to Tartus."

"I did not flee! I was called up to do military service," Yusuf said, trying to duck his responsibility and blame the circumstances.

"No. You ran away. Just like she did. You felt small, you had an inferiority complex regarding the British guy. You should have chased the British guy out of her life."

"Is love just a duel to you, Lamis?" He was aware that he called her 'Lamis' for the first time without adding the polite title "Aniseh" before her name.

"Yes, it is a duel. At least, it was to her. You do not know that she was such a—she is such a fine young woman. She told me about you, about your political involvement. She knew that you and I were of a similar mind. Do you know that after she met you, all of her ideas were turned upside down? She used to come to me and say, 'I always fight with him. You and Yusuf are both extremely intelligent, Lamis.' I knew about her situation. I heard how she had left her family and lived at Fawziya's and the professor's most of the time. I advised her to settle down and analyze the motivations behind her political activities because I knew that her interest stemmed from her difficult situation, from… she was with the English professor. And when I reminded her of this she laughed and said, 'What's stopping me? Aren't you all internationalists?'"

"It was just one of her whims," Yusuf answered.

"No," Lamis said. "Don't you think that she felt she needed an emotional and intellectual escape?"

"Perhaps. It's possible." Yusuf was silent for a moment. "But political involvement is not an escape. It cannot be used as psychological compensation."

It was only then that Lamis erupted. "Dallal was right when she said that you have a harsh and almost inhuman side, and that you always try to cover up what you are really feeling!"

Yusuf did not respond. He felt respectful and friendly affection for Lamis. He started to feel tranquil, profound emotions penetrating into his depths. He did not know how he dared, but he reached out and extended his hand toward hers on top of the table. She blushed, shook her head, and withdrew her hand from the table, saying, "Excuse me—"

Damascus

With the beginning of the new academic year, 1982–1983, a tragic accident befell the family of Chief Sergeant Yunis. On the first day of the school year, little Ali, who was entering the fourth grade, was walking to school when a military vehicle on the road leading to the school hit him. He died instantly.

Chief Sergeant Yunis was now alone with his wife, especially now that Muhammad had failed in school, joined the army, and left the house like Dallal before him. Chief Sergeant Yunis started to feel that his life had been for nothing and that he had almost reached its end to find that he had done nothing. Once again he found himself returning to his final port, his ship broken. Everything in his life had been destroyed, or was far away. Muhsin was still in Russia. Recently, he wrote that he had married a Russian woman and did not know when he would return, maybe in ten years or so... perhaps he would never come back. Or maybe he would go to another Arab country.

All he knew about Dallal was that she was living and working in Britain. He did not know if she would ever want to return. She occasionally sent a few curt postcards, addressing them only to her mother. In them she said that her health was good and that she was working, but she never mentioned coming back.

The death of her brother Ali was what made the chief sergeant forget his wounded pride and ask her mother to write to her requesting her to return. But Dallal did not come. She sent a letter saying that she had not stopped crying for a week and that she could not believe that life could be so cruel. But she gave no indication of returning.

On January 1, 1983, Chief Sergeant Yunis retired after 30 years in the military. He returned to his village, still holding onto his dream of settling down in his birthplace and the land of his youth. The house that he had been building for two years was finally finished, so he lived in it with his wife. His dreams of pruning olive trees and farming and drinking maté with his friends quickly evaporated. Farm work was scarce and his old friends were all now busy with their own jobs. He was used to working and could not spend the whole day sitting at home. He formed a partnership with his brother Muhammad, bought a minibus, and worked on the Tartus–Draykish line. He felt that he needed to work at something or he would die of emptiness.

And so, here Chief Sergeant Yunis was today, driving a bus on a road that he used to travel on foot. He was thinking about his life and what a waste it was, waiting for Muhsin's return, trying to expel Dallal's ghost from within himself, all the time secretly hoping that she would return one day and start her life anew.

He tried in vain to rid Dallal from his mind. To him, Dallal had been transformed into visible sorrow, constant daydreaming, and a deep sadness that did not allow him to be honest with himself. He tried to avoid mentioning her in front of her mother or other people. But he could still hear her voice screaming out deep inside of him, "You hit me, you awful, despicable man!" He felt pain, anger, and sorrow all together, while wondering, "Where did I go wrong in her upbringing? Children these days are not our children. They are the children of schools and the neighborhood. It is true that each generation is different." He pondered this, "She should have tolerated me. I am still her father after all, whether or not we were raised in different times. I forgave her many errors. She should have come back after her anger and mine had cooled down."

"Why did she leave the house? Why did she refuse to see me? My God. Where did I go wrong with her?" he asked himself. Sorrow flooded his heart, the sorrow of someone wounded by the person closest to him. "I tried to raise her the best way I knew how, to bring her up far away from bad influences. I knew the corruption of life in Damascus. I always tried to bring her up without conflicts. I did not impose many responsibilities on her. I never even spoke to her about Yusuf. Isn't it natural that a father should want a nice, stable young man for his daughter? She would not let me wish for anything. The guy himself was polite; he never even broached the topic with me, never crossed the boundaries of politeness and friendly relations. It is natural that a father should desire the best for his children."

He pulled his bus up next to a coffee shop and went inside, thinking all the while. "When will Muhsin return? *Inshallah*, he will return before I die. Muhammad is doing all right in the military. *Inshallah*, Dallal will return. Oh, poor little Ali... what did Dallal do when she heard about Ali's death? He loved her and she used to spoil him. *Inshallah*, she will return. Come back or not come back—to hell with it! She is alone in London. How does she live, I wonder? Does she not think about us—her father or her mother or her brothers? Dallal is not like her mother in that way. Khadija is a tender woman.

"To be brought up well is not enough these days; children are brought up by school, movies, and the neighborhood. They are raised by television and not at home. I will sell the house in Damascus and finish with the final thing that binds me to the city that sucked the life and youth out of me. That city destroyed my family. It killed my little boy, made my daughter homeless, and led Muhammad astray with its distractions. I will go to Damascus next week, sell the house, and buy an olive grove with the profits. The price of houses is going up these days. No, wait. Maybe it would be better to buy a house in Tartus—to buy a clinic and prepare it for Muhsin's return to Syria. Who knows when Muhsin will return? Will he work in Tartus or will he settle down in Damascus when he comes? It is better to leave him the house in Damascus—he is used to it. He will decide where he wants to live in the future. It's better to—"

"Hello, Uncle Abu Muhsin." Though daydreaming, Chief Sergeant Yunis heard a voice greeting him. The coffee shop was in the square near the bus station in Draykish where he was waiting for his bus to fill with passengers to take to Tartus. He knew the speaker's voice. He looked up. "Yusuf, Ustaz Yusuf! Hello there, how are you? What are you doing here? Please, sit down—"

He got up and gave Yusuf a big hug, then ordered him a cup of coffee. "*Ahlan wa Sahlan*! It's been a long time—a very long time—since we've seen you."

"It's true. And you, what are you doing here?" asked Yusuf, who was also surprised by Yunis' presence in the coffee shop.

"Oh, well, I retired and came back to the village. Now I drive that minibus." The chief sergeant pointed to a white mini-van parked at the bus stop across the square.

"The one going to Tartus?" asked Yusuf.

"Yes, yes. So, what's happened to you? We never see you anymore. What are you doing here?" Yunis' questions rushed out. How much he cared for Yusuf, how much he missed him!

"I came to take care of some bureaucratic paperwork. I'm

going to transfer my official residency papers to Damascus and settle down there. I've moved from Yabrud to Damascus."

"You found a house in Damascus? You must have good luck! Where are you living?"

"I haven't found a house yet," Yusuf said. "But in the meantime I'm staying with a friend of mine. What ever happened to your house in Mezzeh?"

An idea suddenly crossed Yunis's mind. "Yusuf, we are family. I will rent you the house on one condition—that you give it back to me when Muhsin returns from Russia. If he decides to live in Damascus, of course. You know you are like a son to me, like Muhsin." The chief sergeant was quiet for a moment. "But you were thinking about returning to Tartus and living there. What happened to you? Has Damascus put a spell on you?" Remembering Dallal, he smiled. "I mean, has one of the beautiful young women in Damascus put a spell on you?"

Yusuf reached to pick up his coffee cup and smiled, remembering Lamis al-Muradi.

But the smile left the chief sergeant's face. "I wish you the best of luck in Damascus, Ustaz Yusuf. As for me, well, it destroyed my family. Maybe your generation's luck—yours and Muhsin's—will be better than our generation's luck."

Whenever Yunis thought about his son Muhsin, Dallal immediately popped into his mind. He wished that Yusuf would ask about her; Yusuf would definitely have had news of her.

Yusuf too was thinking about Dallal and wishing he could ask her father how she was doing, but he was not brave enough.

Neither Yunis nor Yusuf could say her name out loud.

"Come on! Come with me, Ustaz Yusuf. Let's go, the van is full."

Yusuf walked toward the van, got in, and sat next to the window thinking about Yunis' dreams and his own dreams. He thought about his life, the days he had seen, the people he had known in Tartus, Hassakeh, and Yabrud. He thought about war and the army, teaching, love, and philosophy. About Yunis, Dallal, Muhsin, Ali, and Umm Muhsin, about Lamis al-Muradi, Fawziya Sabbagh, Minerva, Zuhayr, and Morton White and—and—and...

He looked out the window at the olive trees scattered at the foot of the mountain, encircling the mountain road. "Another life cycle," he whispered to himself. He recalled a quotation from Galileo that he never tired of repeating to his students, "Despite all this, it still goes around." He shook his head and muttered in an audible voice as though he were lecturing, "Despite all this, it still goes around. It goes around."

Out the window were oaks and medlars, olive and oak trees, terebinth and carob trees all standing along the side of the road. Groups of trees were gathered here and there, spread out around the foot of the mountain. He turned his glance to the foot of the mountain where it approached the valley and saw the Qays river twisting and bending between two valleys toward the point where it emptied out into the sea. He remembered a saying from the Torah, "All rivers flow into the sea. The sea is never full." He kept thinking about Yunis, his life, his dreams, his current situation, and what would happen to him.

He thought to himself, "It goes around and around. Is there a new cycle for this cursed time we live in, or is it just like all the other cycles? It goes around and around. But in the end it keeps going by, no matter how it twists, no matter how it bends. It goes by and then flows out to the sea. It goes by just like, just like—just like this river. It goes by just like life. It goes by again and again. And we go by with it."

Translators' Afterword

Just Like a River (Hakadha ka-l nahar) is the first novel of the prominent Syrian cultural and intellectual figure Muhammad Kamil al-Khatib. Originally from the Syrian coastal town of Tartus, Khatib currently lives and works in Damascus. He has written six books of criticism, three scholarly studies, six collections of short stories, and four novels—the most recent of which was published this year. Khatib is a member of what in Syria is referred to as the *Jeel al-Thawra*, the "Revolutionary Generation," or *Jeel al-Sitteenat*, the "Sixties Generation," a group of Syrians profoundly affected by the loss of Palestine, the rise of Arab nationalism and socialism, Gamal Abdel Nasser, the international context of the Cold War, and the other political and intellectual upheavals of the period in Syria and the Arab world. The rise to power of the Ba'ath party in the 1960s and Hafez al-Asad, another member of this generation who went on to become the leader of the party and president of Syria, also profoundly changed Syria and the region. The impact of these events on Khatib's perspective on Syrian and Arab society informs and suffuses all his writings and this novel in particular.

In *Just Like a River*, which originally came out in 1984, Khatib uses a social-realist style, like many other Arab novelists of his generation. The novel's brilliance resides in both its precise reflection of its specific time and place—the 1980s in Syria—but also in its lasting relevance. Although the specific details of the novel are sure to strike a note with anyone who knows Syria, particularly the Syria of that era, the novel is still relevant today as a Syrian novel within the larger Arab context—and indeed universally. The kinds of details that are captured so precisely—the anxiety of young people about the future, the decision to live in the village or the city, or, more drastically, whether to emigrate or not, the lack of jobs for university-educated people, and the difficulty of men and women to form relationships—are an uncannily accurate depiction of today's Syria, just as they were of the Syria of this earlier period. *Just Like a River* is a good representation of Khatib's unrelenting critical eye that so keenly notices details and never shies away from representing the truth about society, culture, and politics, however difficult that may be.

The specific period in which this novel is set, the early 1980s, is remembered as the period of the missile crisis in Syria and Lebanon, when Syria's conflict with Israel escalated and there was fear of an all-out war. This possibility of war is key to understanding the mood and the plot of the text, in that the characters in the novel bring up the issue frequently—for example, when Yusuf, Dallal, and her father all discuss what will happen, when Yusuf is called up by the military, and when his friend Ahmad Abbud pays the government to be released from his call-up. This period was extremely important in Syria for determining its role and status in today's geopolitical context. Again, though this specific political and military crisis dates the novel, it is striking how it is seemingly being replayed again today in 2002.

This resonance is perhaps part of the reason that the Syrian landscape drawn by Khatib strikes such a deep chord with Syrian readers. Indeed, anyone who has lived in Syria, particularly Damascus, will immediately recognize the locations that fill his characters' lives. The specificity of place is layered into his work through the films at the Kindi theater, shopping at the Nuri bookshop, the *servees* station for Mezzeh, Thursday night dinner and drinking at the Vendôme restaurant, coffee at the Dar and Ya Marhaba cafés, the walks on the corniche in Tartus and the tree-filled coastal villages. Though much of Khatib's focus is on Damascus and the Syrian coast, he also includes characters from a variety of locations: the Assyrian character Minerva who is from the rural Jezira area in northeastern Syria, for example, and Lamis al-Muradi, the young woman who leaves Syria to earn money for her family in Kuwait.

Khatib's evocations of the coast are not merely a nostalgic device recalling the area of his childhood, but rather function more symbolically. The family of Chief Sergeant Yunis, for example, in many ways serves as a microcosm of Syrian society through its various members. This family is representative of a large number of people from the coastal region, who joined the army as a means of gaining upward social mobility and came to Damascus in search of a better education and life for their children. Chief Sergeant Yunis's despair at the end of the novel is shown through the fate of his four children—his beloved youngest son Ali dead of a car accident, a symbol of modernity and the dangers of urban life; his oldest son Muhsin living in Russia and married to a Russian woman; his only daughter Dallal estranged and living in London; and his remaining son Muhammad a high school dropout who joined the army and does not feel there is any hope for his future. Yunis's return to the coast to drive a *servees* between Tartus and Draykish is far from how he planned his retirement in his village, just as his children's futures are far from what he had dreamed and expected for them. Though his reaction to Yusuf's decision not to return to live in the village seems optimistic and upbeat, Yunis's wish that Yusuf not end up like him is coupled with the overarching theme of the novel—a river always flows to the sea as part of its continuous life-cycle. And this perspective does not leave the reader with much optimism about the prospects for Yusuf and Muhsin's generation.

The movement of people from the country to the city, here mainly represented by Syrian coastal villagers who converge on Damascus, is one of the most important themes in the novel and is paralleled by a similar move by Syrians out of the country. Whether they flee like Dallal, leave to study like Muhsin, or work abroad temporarily like Lamis, the increasingly limited options within Syria caused a flood of people to leave the country in the 1980s and beyond, just as they had left their villages before. Once again, the very specific and detailed Syrian situation has relevance in a regional and global context. The continued expansion of the city and the burgeoning suburbs that have been continually springing up in Damascus since even before the 1980s is paralleled in urban centers throughout the world. The explosion of urban locations due to the increasing 'inner immigration' by people from the countryside to ever-expanding cities is one of the most important phenomena affecting the third world, a theme that is reflected in much world literature, particularly that of Asia, Africa, and Latin America.

This urban migration is merely one of many themes the novel takes up. Khatib also explores, for example, the alienation of the youth of the country, the increase in education and the lack of opportunities for these educated people, the continual local and regional insecurity because of ongoing political tensions and the threat of war with Israel, the ways in which communities and families constitute and reconstitute themselves and how this is understood in the context of other social changes, the struggle between the generations—that between fathers and daughters is the most striking and poignant example in this novel—and the way in which relationships between men and women are understood and lived out in these conditions. The constraints of time and space that limit these characters and their lives is powerfully represented throughout the novel.

Khatib's brilliance in this novel also partly resides in the devastatingly accurate portrayals of his characters, each of whom is profoundly flawed, and therefore human, but with whom the reader cannot but empathize. The reader agonizes as Dallal and Yusuf have conversation after conversation that seems doomed to lead to disaster, although it is patently obvious that each loves the other and simply does not know how to begin to express this. The misunderstandings between family members, such as the tension that ultimately builds to the breaking point between Dallal and her father, leading to their fight and her flight to London, are drawn so clearly and so convincingly that though the reader may choose a side, it is clear that the author is able painstakingly to show the inner feelings and struggles of both parties to the dispute.

It is this at-times-painful ambiguity and social critique that makes *Just Like a River* a successful novel. Though it may seem at first glance that each of the characters in this work could be read as a 'type' or a mere symbol, as the details build the story, it is clear how each is profoundly complex and complicated. Through these portraits and the way in which they interconnect through the plot of the work, Khatib explores the depth of confusion in human emotions and actions, while continuously insisting on the political and social context of their lives.

Because this text is so rooted in the local, in the complex

and subtle textures of Syrian culture, society, and politics, we faced many dilemmas as translators. The act of translation is well described by the same metaphor used by Muhammad Kamil al-Khatib in the title of this novel, *Just Like a River*, perhaps more so when two translators work together. The circuitous path followed by the translators from a complete Arabic novel to its translated English version often seemed to be flowing in different directions, at different speeds, sometimes coming very near the point from which it originated, and leading to various places along the way before ultimately pouring into the sea as a complete translation. By working together as the co-translators of this novel, we hope that we have produced what is, in the end, a better translation through this process of give-and-take. As a Syrian native speaker of Arabic and an American native speaker of English who studies Arabic, both of whom share a love of Arabic literature, we hope our partnership will bring this literary work, the first of al-Khatib's novels to be published in English, to a broader readership.

The decision to translate this particular novel arose out of one of our many discussions about contemporary Syrian literature when we both were living in Syria in the 1990s. Michelle asked Maher what one book he felt had the greatest impact on him and that he thought was the most important to his generation. Without hesitation he lent her his copy of *Just Like a River*. Shortly afterward, we decided to translate it together. The translation took shape not only through discussions about Syrian culture, society, and literature, through which we entered the mental space of the characters and their lives, but also physically in the spaces where the novel itself is set. We began work on the project in Damascus, just above the streets Yusuf and Zuhayr walk together at night discussing Zuhayr's typology of prostitutes. Over one long weekend, we took our work to the coast and sat and translated on the seaside, driving through the roads that Chief Sergeant Yunis passes through daily at the end of the novel as a *servees* driver. We sat in the seaside cafés that Yusuf frequented while deciding whether or not to make his move to Damascus permanent, giving up his dream of returning to his village and Tartus one day. Michelle was studying at the university where Dallal and Fawziyya studied, though her trajectory and experiences were very different as an American sitting in classes about Arabic literature, rather than a Syrian studying English literature. Upon leaving Damascus, the translation then moved to Britain, like Dallal at the end of the novel, before it was finalized in North America, between Ottawa and New York City.

We hope to have presented English-language readers with a text that is readable and enjoyable, but also acknowledges the fact that it is indeed translated, and that the language, the precise expressions and phrases employed by Khatib in Arabic, are able the same in English. Although in this Afterword we have mainly concentrated on drawing out some of the ideas contained in Khatib's text, we would also like to give the reader a feeling of the artistry of his succinct use of the Arabic language. Khatib writes in *fusha*, the Arabic literary language conventionally used by novelists, poets, and other authors, but his simple style often comes close to the Arabic language spoken by people on a daily basis, especially in the dialogue between his characters. Though his style and language is not high-flown, the novel itself is far from simple, and it is this complexity and layering that we hope the English-language reader will discern through our translation. In order to preserve some sense of the Arabic original we have left several words untranslated throughout the text and also pointed to certain uses of language within the translated English itself.

This novel is being published in this translation in a time when many critics and writers are discussing the ways in which Arab writers, like writers of other languages considered "marginal" in the European and North American contexts, have been driven to write for translation, that is, to produce books that will sell well in English translation. The publication of *Just Like a River* is striking in this context; not only was it not written for translation, but indeed the author himself seemed perplexed (though always generous and positive) when we approached him for permission to translate it, saying that it was a work that was written in Arabic for an Arab readership. We would like therefore to acknowledge the warm and kind support of Muhammad Kamil al-Khatib and thank him for allowing us to translate his novel and bring this work of Arabic fiction, set in Syria and infused with a Syrian consciousness, to an English-reading audience. Ultimately, we are confident that this work will resonate with an English-language readership because it is after all a human story, one of people's complex emotions and relationships to themselves, others, and the events surrounding them.

Glossary

Abu: Common form of address of a father followed by the name of his oldest son.

Ahlan: Common greeting meaning "hello."

Ahlan wa sahlan: Hello and/or welcome.

Aniseh: lit. Miss. This is a polite and formal term attached to a woman's first name. Used to address teachers and young women in general to express respect.

Awlad haram: Bad people. Here, Dallal's father is warning her about the dangers of life in a big city like Damascus and that she must beware of people who may try to take advantage of her.

Maté: A bitter tea originating in South America. Brought to Syria by Syrians who had worked in South America. It is prepared by pouring hot water over a tea leaf mixture and is drunk through a straw with holes in the end that acts as a filter. How it is drunk varies from region to region, though the preparation and consumption of maté is almost ritualistic. The drink is particularly popular among people from the coast and the south.

Inshallah: lit. If God is willing. This expression is commonly used in speech in Arabic. Here, it most often expresses a wish that something will happen.

Servees: Shared taxis that drive along a route to a certain destination making stops on the way. In the 1980s these began being replaced by larger vehicles like mini-vans that are called micro-buses.

Sindiyana: lit. evergreen oak. Particularly common in the coastal regions of Syria, these large oak trees were often planted at the burial sites of Alawi shaykhs.

Sitt: lit. Lady. This is a polite term of address used for women of any age, irrespective of their marital status.

Tenekeh: A container in which olive oil is stored, approximately the size of a barrel.

Umm: Common form of address of a mother followed by the name of her oldest son.

Ustaz: lit. Professor. This is a polite term used to address both a teacher and a young man, especially one educated or in the process of become educated.